ROBERT F. KENNEDY

ROBERT F. KENNEDY

Daniel J. Petrillo

CHELSEA HOUSE PUBLISHERS
NEW YORK
PHILADELPHIA

Chelsea House Publishers
EDITOR-IN-CHIEF: Nancy Toff
EXECUTIVE EDITOR: Remmel T. Nunn
MANAGING EDITOR: Karyn Gullen Browne
COPY CHIEF: Juliann Barbato
PICTURE EDITOR: Adrian G. Allen
ART DIRECTOR: Maria Epes
MANUFACTURING MANAGER: Gerald Levine

World Leaders—Past & Present
SENIOR EDITOR: John W. Selfridge

Staff for ROBERT F. KENNEDY
ASSOCIATE EDITOR: Sean Dolan
COPY EDITOR: Karen Hammonds
DEPUTY COPY CHIEF: Ellen Scordato
EDITORIAL ASSISTANT: Heather Lewis
PICTURE RESEARCHERS: Elie Porter and Karen Herman
ASSISTANT ART DIRECTOR: Laurie Jewell
DESIGNER: David Murray
PRODUCTION COORDINATOR: Joseph Romano
COVER ILLUSTRATION: Kye Carbone

First Printing

1 3 5 7 9 8 6 4 2

Library of Congress Cataloging in Publication Data

Petrillo, Daniel J. 1941–
Robert F. Kennedy / Daniel J. Petrillo.

p. cm.—(World leaders past & present)
Bibliography: p.
Includes index.
Summary: Traces the life of the attorney general and senator who
was assassinated while campaigning for the Democratic presidential
nomination in 1968.

ISBN 1-55546-840-3
      0-7910-0581-X (pbk.)

1. Kennedy, Robert F., 1925–1968—Juvenile literature.
2. Legislators—United States—Biography—Juvenile
literature. 3. United States. Congress. Senate—Biography—
Juvenile literature. [1. Kennedy, Robert F., 1925–1968. 2.
Legislators.] I. Title. II. Series.
E840.8.K4R46   1989   88-14889
973.922′092′4 — dc19   CIP
[B]   AC

Contents

JOHN ADAMS
JOHN QUINCY ADAMS
KONRAD ADENAUER
ALEXANDER THE GREAT
SALVADOR ALLENDE
MARC ANTONY
CORAZON AQUINO
YASIR ARAFAT
KING ARTHUR
HAFEZ al-ASSAD
KEMAL ATATÜRK
ATTILA
CLEMENT ATTLEE
AUGUSTUS CAESAR
MENACHEM BEGIN
DAVID BEN-GURION
OTTO VON BISMARCK
LÉON BLUM
SIMON BOLÍVAR
CESARE BORGIA
WILLY BRANDT
LEONID BREZHNEV
JULIUS CAESAR
JOHN CALVIN
JIMMY CARTER
FIDEL CASTRO
CATHERINE THE GREAT
CHARLEMAGNE
CHIANG KAI-SHEK
WINSTON CHURCHILL
GEORGES CLEMENCEAU
CLEOPATRA
CONSTANTINE THE GREAT
HERNÁN CORTÉS
OLIVER CROMWELL
GEORGES-JACQUES
   DANTON
JEFFERSON DAVIS
MOSHE DAYAN
CHARLES DE GAULLE
EAMON DE VALERA
EUGENE DEBS
DENG XIAOPING
BENJAMIN DISRAELI
ALEXANDER DUBČEK
FRANÇOIS & JEAN-CLAUDE
   DUVALIER
DWIGHT EISENHOWER
ELEANOR OF AQUITAINE
ELIZABETH I
FAISAL
FERDINAND & ISABELLA
FRANCISCO FRANCO
BENJAMIN FRANKLIN

FREDERICK THE GREAT
INDIRA GANDHI
MOHANDAS GANDHI
GIUSEPPE GARIBALDI
AMIN & BASHIR GEMAYEL
GENGHIS KHAN
WILLIAM GLADSTONE
MIKHAIL GORBACHEV
ULYSSES S. GRANT
ERNESTO "CHE" GUEVARA
TENZIN GYATSO
ALEXANDER HAMILTON
DAG HAMMARSKJÖLD
HENRY VIII
HENRY OF NAVARRE
PAUL VON HINDENBURG
HIROHITO
ADOLF HITLER
HO CHI MINH
KING HUSSEIN
IVAN THE TERRIBLE
ANDREW JACKSON
JAMES I
WOJCIECH JARUZELSKI
THOMAS JEFFERSON
JOAN OF ARC
POPE JOHN XXIII
POPE JOHN PAUL II
LYNDON JOHNSON
BENITO JUÁREZ
JOHN KENNEDY
ROBERT KENNEDY
JOMO KENYATTA
AYATOLLAH KHOMEINI
NIKITA KHRUSHCHEV
KIM IL SUNG
MARTIN LUTHER KING, JR.
HENRY KISSINGER
KUBLAI KHAN
LAFAYETTE
ROBERT E. LEE
VLADIMIR LENIN
ABRAHAM LINCOLN
DAVID LLOYD GEORGE
LOUIS XIV
MARTIN LUTHER
JUDAS MACCABEUS
JAMES MADISON
NELSON & WINNIE
   MANDELA
MAO ZEDONG
FERDINAND MARCOS
GEORGE MARSHALL

MARY, QUEEN OF SCOTS
TOMÁŠ MASARYK
GOLDA MEIR
KLEMENS VON METTERNICH
JAMES MONROE
HOSNI MUBARAK
ROBERT MUGABE
BENITO MUSSOLINI
NAPOLÉON BONAPARTE
GAMAL ABDEL NASSER
JAWAHARLAL NEHRU
NERO
NICHOLAS II
RICHARD NIXON
KWAME NKRUMAH
DANIEL ORTEGA
MOHAMMED REZA PAHLAVI
THOMAS PAINE
CHARLES STEWART
   PARNELL
PERICLES
JUAN PERÓN
PETER THE GREAT
POL POT
MUAMMAR EL-QADDAFI
RONALD REAGAN
CARDINAL RICHELIEU
MAXIMILIEN ROBESPIERRE
ELEANOR ROOSEVELT
FRANKLIN ROOSEVELT
THEODORE ROOSEVELT
ANWAR SADAT
HAILE SELASSIE
PRINCE SIHANOUK
JAN SMUTS
JOSEPH STALIN
SUKARNO
SUN YAT-SEN
TAMERLANE
MOTHER TERESA
MARGARET THATCHER
JOSIP BROZ TITO
TOUSSAINT L'OUVERTURE
LEON TROTSKY
PIERRE TRUDEAU
HARRY TRUMAN
QUEEN VICTORIA
LECH WALESA
GEORGE WASHINGTON
CHAIM WEIZMANN
WOODROW WILSON
XERXES
EMILIANO ZAPATA
ZHOU ENLAI

CHELSEA HOUSE PUBLISHERS

ON LEADERSHIP

Arthur M. Schlesinger, jr.

LEADERSHIP, it may be said, is really what makes the world go round. Love no doubt smooths the passage; but love is a private transaction between consenting adults. Leadership is a public transaction with history. The idea of leadership affirms the capacity of individuals to move, inspire, and mobilize masses of people so that they act together in pursuit of an end. Sometimes leadership serves good purposes, sometimes bad; but whether the end is benign or evil, great leaders are those men and women who leave their personal stamp on history.

Now, the very concept of leadership implies the proposition that individuals can make a difference. This proposition has never been universally accepted. From classical times to the present day, eminent thinkers have regarded individuals as no more than the agents and pawns of larger forces, whether the gods and goddesses of the ancient world or, in the modern era, race, class, nation, the dialectic, the will of the people, the spirit of the times, history itself. Against such forces, the individual dwindles into insignificance.

So contends the thesis of historical determinism. Tolstoy's great novel *War and Peace* offers a famous statement of the case. Why, Tolstoy asked, did millions of men in the Napoleonic Wars, denying their human feelings and their common sense, move back and forth across Europe slaughtering their fellows? "The war," Tolstoy answered, "was bound to happen simply because it was bound to happen." All prior history predetermined it. As for leaders, they, Tolstoy said, "are but the labels that serve to give a name to an end and, like labels, they have the least possible connection with the event." The greater the leader, "the more conspicuous the inevitability and the predestination of every act he commits." The leader, said Tolstoy, is "the slave of history."

Determinism takes many forms. Marxism is the determinism of class. Nazism the determinism of race. But the idea of men and women as the slaves of history runs athwart the deepest human instincts. Rigid determinism abolishes the idea of human freedom—

the assumption of free choice that underlies every move we make, every word we speak, every thought we think. It abolishes the idea of human responsibility, since it is manifestly unfair to reward or punish people for actions that are by definition beyond their control. No one can live consistently by any deterministic creed. The Marxist states prove this themselves by their extreme susceptibility to the cult of leadership.

More than that, history refutes the idea that individuals make no difference. In December 1931 a British politician crossing Park Avenue in New York City between 76th and 77th Streets around 10:30 P.M. looked in the wrong direction and was knocked down by an automobile—a moment, he later recalled, of a man aghast, a world aglare: "I do not understand why I was not broken like an eggshell or squashed like a gooseberry." Fourteen months later an American politician, sitting in an open car in Miami, Florida, was fired on by an assassin; the man beside him was hit. Those who believe that individuals make no difference to history might well ponder whether the next two decades would have been the same had Mario Constasino's car killed Winston Churchill in 1931 and Giuseppe Zangara's bullet killed Franklin Roosevelt in 1933. Suppose, in addition, that Adolf Hitler had been killed in the street fighting during the Munich *Putsch* of 1923 and that Lenin had died of typhus during World War I. What would the 20th century be like now?

For better or for worse, individuals do make a difference. "The notion that a people can run itself and its affairs anonymously," wrote the philosopher William James, "is now well known to be the silliest of absurdities. Mankind does nothing save through initiatives on the part of inventors, great or small, and imitation by the rest of us—these are the sole factors in human progress. Individuals of genius show the way, and set the patterns, which common people then adopt and follow."

Leadership, James suggests, means leadership in thought as well as in action. In the long run, leaders in thought may well make the greater difference to the world. But, as Woodrow Wilson once said, "Those only are leaders of men, in the general eye, who lead in action. . . . It is at their hands that new thought gets its translation into the crude language of deeds." Leaders in thought often invent in solitude and obscurity, leaving to later generations the tasks of imitation. Leaders in action—the leaders portrayed in this series—have to be effective in their own time.

And they cannot be effective by themselves. They must act in response to the rhythms of their age. Their genius must be adapted, in a phrase of William James's, "to the receptivities of the moment." Leaders are useless without followers. "There goes the mob," said the French politician hearing a clamor in the streets. "I am their leader. I must follow them." Great leaders turn the inchoate emotions of the mob to purposes of their own. They seize on the opportunities of their time, the hopes, fears, frustrations, crises, potentialities. They succeed when events have prepared the way for them, when the community is awaiting to be aroused, when they can provide the clarifying and organizing ideas. Leadership ignites the circuit between the individual and the mass and thereby alters history.

It may alter history for better or for worse. Leaders have been responsible for the most extravagant follies and most monstrous crimes that have beset suffering humanity. They have also been vital in such gains as humanity has made in individual freedom, religious and racial tolerance, social justice, and respect for human rights.

There is no sure way to tell in advance who is going to lead for good and who for evil. But a glance at the gallery of men and women in *World Leaders—Past and Present* suggests some useful tests.

One test is this: Do leaders lead by force or by persuasion? By command or by consent? Through most of history leadership was exercised by the divine right of authority. The duty of followers was to defer and to obey. "Theirs not to reason why / Theirs but to do and die." On occasion, as with the so-called enlightened despots of the 18th century in Europe, absolutist leadership was animated by humane purposes. More often, absolutism nourished the passion for domination, land, gold, and conquest and resulted in tyranny.

The great revolution of modern times has been the revolution of equality. The idea that all people should be equal in their legal condition has undermined the old structure of authority, hierarchy, and deference. The revolution of equality has had two contrary effects on the nature of leadership. For equality, as Alexis de Tocqueville pointed out in his great study *Democracy in America*, might mean equality in servitude as well as equality in freedom.

"I know of only two methods of establishing equality in the political world," Tocqueville wrote. "Rights must be given to every citizen, or none at all to anyone . . . save one, who is the master of all." There was no middle ground "between the sovereignty of all and the absolute power of one man." In his astonishing prediction

9

of 20th-century totalitarian dictatorship, Tocqueville explained how the revolution of equality could lead to the *"Führerprinzip"* and more terrible absolutism than the world had ever known.

But when rights are given to every citizen and the sovereignty of all is established, the problem of leadership takes a new form, becomes more exacting than ever before. It is easy to issue commands and enforce them by the rope and the stake, the concentration camp and the *gulag.* It is much harder to use argument and achievement to overcome opposition and win consent. The Founding Fathers of the United States understood the difficulty. They believed that history had given them the opportunity to decide, as Alexander Hamilton wrote in the first Federalist Paper, whether men are indeed capable of basing government on "reflection and choice, or whether they are forever destined to depend . . . on accident and force."

Government by reflection and choice called for a new style of leadership and a new quality of followership. It required leaders to be responsive to popular concerns, and it required followers to be active and informed participants in the process. Democracy does not eliminate emotion from politics; sometimes it fosters demagoguery; but it is confident that, as the greatest of democratic leaders put it, you cannot fool all of the people all of the time. It measures leadership by results and retires those who overreach or falter or fail.

It is true that in the long run despots are measured by results too. But they can postpone the day of judgment, sometimes indefinitely, and in the meantime they can do infinite harm. It is also true that democracy is no guarantee of virtue and intelligence in government, for the voice of the people is not necessarily the voice of God. But democracy, by assuring the right of opposition, offers built-in resistance to the evils inherent in absolutism. As the theologian Reinhold Niebuhr summed it up, "Man's capacity for justice makes democracy possible, but man's inclination to injustice makes democracy necessary."

A second test for leadership is the end for which power is sought. When leaders have as their goal the supremacy of a master race or the promotion of totalitarian revolution or the acquisition and exploitation of colonies or the protection of greed and privilege or the preservation of personal power, it is likely that their leadership will do little to advance the cause of humanity. When their goal is the abolition of slavery, the liberation of women, the enlargement of opportunity for the poor and powerless, the extension of equal rights to racial minorities, the defense of the freedoms of expression and opposition, it is likely that their leadership will increase the sum of human liberty and welfare.

Leaders have done great harm to the world. They have also conferred great benefits. You will find both sorts in this series. Even "good" leaders must be regarded with a certain wariness. Leaders are not demigods; they put on their trousers one leg after another just like ordinary mortals. No leader is infallible, and every leader needs to be reminded of this at regular intervals. Irreverence irritates leaders but is their salvation. Unquestioning submission corrupts leaders and demeans followers. Making a cult of a leader is always a mistake. Fortunately hero worship generates its own antidote. "Every hero," said Emerson, "becomes a bore at last."

The signal benefit the great leaders confer is to embolden the rest of us to live according to our own best selves, to be active, insistent, and resolute in affirming our own sense of things. For great leaders attest to the reality of human freedom against the supposed inevitabilities of history. And they attest to the wisdom and power that may lie within the most unlikely of us, which is why Abraham Lincoln remains the supreme example of great leadership. A great leader, said Emerson, exhibits new possibilities to all humanity. "We feed on genius. . . . Great men exist that there may be greater men."

Great leaders, in short, justify themselves by emancipating and empowering their followers. So humanity struggles to master its destiny, remembering with Alexis de Tocqueville: "It is true that around every man a fatal circle is traced beyond which he cannot pass; but within the wide verge of that circle he is powerful and free; as it is with man, so with communities."

1

Champion of the Dispossessed

It was just before midnight on June 4, 1968, when the candidate addressed the crowd in the Embassy Room of the Ambassador Hotel in Los Angeles, California, where a jubilant and enthusiastic throng had gathered to celebrate Robert Kennedy's victory in the just concluded California Democratic presidential primary. After months of indecision by Kennedy as to the wisdom of challenging the incumbent president, Lyndon B. Johnson, for his party's nomination, the campaign had gotten off to a late start. His hesitancy had cost Kennedy the support of much of his natural constituency — opponents of the United States's involvement in the ongoing war in Vietnam. As senator from New York, Kennedy had been among the first congressmen to speak out against the Johnson administration's Vietnam policy, but when he could not decide whether to take on Johnson, another antiwar senator, Eugene McCarthy of Minnesota, seized the moment. McCarthy's unlikely campaign — conventional wisdom deemed it political suicide to challenge a sitting president for his party's nomination — captured the imagination of the war's opponents. College students were particularly attracted to McCarthy.

> *So many people have him [Kennedy] absolutely wrong. They think he is cold, calculating, ruthless. Actually he is hot-blooded, romantic, compassionate.*
> —JOSEPH ALSOP
> columnist

Senator Robert F. Kennedy of New York investigates conditions in a tenement on the Lower East Side of Manhattan in May 1967. Kennedy's belief that President Lyndon Johnson was abandoning social programs aimed at the poor was one factor in his decision to seek the presidency in 1968.

A jubilant Kennedy greets his supporters at Los Angeles's Ambassador Hotel following his victory in the California Democratic primary on June 4, 1968. Although Kennedy still trailed Vice-president Hubert Humphrey in the delegate count, his party's nomination for president seemed within his reach.

Hundreds flocked to New Hampshire, site of the first presidential primary, to campaign for him. Radio advertisements asked the Granite State's voters how they would feel "to wake up Wednesday morning to find out that Gene McCarthy had won the New Hampshire primary — to find that New Hampshire had changed the course of American politics."

When the polls closed on Tuesday night, March 12, 1968, McCarthy backers indeed had reason for such contemplation. The president had earned 49.5 percent of the votes to 42.4 percent for McCarthy. More important, McCarthy had won 20 of the 24 delegates to the party's nominating convention, to be held in Chicago in August, and the results were interpreted as a resounding defeat for Johnson and an indication of the strength of the antiwar sentiment among Democrats.

That Saturday, March 16, Robert Kennedy officially entered the race. In the eyes of McCarthy backers and others, the timing of his announcement gave new credence to the charges that had dogged him throughout his political career. It was said that he was ruthless and motivated only by personal ambition, that as the younger brother of the slain John F. Kennedy, who had preceded Johnson as president, he believed he had some sort of familial right to the presidency. McCarthy's supporters charged that Kennedy had lacked the courage to challenge the president directly and had opportunistically entered the race only when McCarthy demonstrated that Johnson could be beaten. Although McCarthyites were overjoyed by their candidate's strong showing, few suspected that he had landed a knockout blow. On the night of March 31, Johnson ended a televised nationwide address on Vietnam by announcing that he would not seek reelection.

Hubert Humphrey (left) secured the Democratic nomination for president in August 1968. He is shown here with Senator Eugene McCarthy of Minnesota, the antiwar candidate whose strong showing in the New Hampshire primary had helped force Johnson to withdraw from the race.

McCarthy's candidacy had been conceived as essentially a one-issue campaign, a protest against the American policy in Vietnam, but Kennedy believed that the war was only one of a number of serious problems facing the United States. He emphasized that America was becoming a nation divided, not only by differences in opinion over what course to pursue in Vietnam but by the violent unrest in predominantly black ghettoes that had exploded in each of the previous three summers. The report of the Kerner Commission on Civil Disorder, a commission appointed by Johnson to investigate the violence, had warned that the split was occurring on racial lines, but in his campaign speeches Kennedy noted time and again that the poverty that engulfed Mexican Americans, Puerto Ricans, Indians, and poor whites, as well as blacks and other minorities, threatened to consign all these individuals to what the economist Michael Harrington called the "Other America." Harrington's book by that title decried the existence of such entrenched

Kennedy's concern with the poor brought him to the Mississippi Delta in May 1967. Shocked by the living conditions there, he said, "My God, I didn't know this sort of thing existed. How can a nation like this allow it?"

poverty in the midst of so much affluence — affluence that allowed poverty to remain invisible to the majority of Americans. Published in 1962, *The Other America* had alerted John Kennedy to the problem of poverty in the United States and had borne fruit in the legislative programs enacted under Johnson known as the War on Poverty. Six years later, Robert Kennedy asserted that not all that much had changed. He warned that the rioting in black urban neighborhoods represented not lawlessness but a cry of rage over inadequate housing, high unemployment, substandard educational facilities and medical care, poor nutrition, high mortality rates, and all the other pernicious legacies of entrenched poverty. At every campaign stop he told his audiences of the unspeakable living conditions he had witnessed firsthand in New York City's Bedford-Stuyvesant and Harlem, on Indian reservations in South Dakota, among the predominantly Mexican-American agricultural workers in California's lettuce and grape fields, in the black communities of Mississippi, in migrant labor camps in New York. Time after time he recounted his stories, recited his statistics, and stated, "I do not find that satisfactory."

Impressed by Kennedy's support of the civil rights movement and his visits to the Mississippi Delta, the civil rights leader Charles Evers (second from right) characterized the senator from New York as the only white politician blacks could trust. In 1969 Evers became the first freely elected black mayor of a Mississippi town since Reconstruction.

> *I do not lightly dismiss the dangers and difficulties of challenging an incumbent President; but these are not ordinary times and this is not an ordinary election. At stake is not simply the leadership of our party or even our country— it is our right to moral leadership on this planet.*
> —ROBERT KENNEDY
> announcing his candidacy
> for president

It was a message many Americans did not want to hear. Believing that recent federal legislation had safeguarded essential legal and political rights, many whites were simply unable to comprehend the continued frustration and rage of blacks and were frightened and angered by the rioting that took place during the "long, hot summers." Even within the Johnson administration, whose leader the prominent black writer Ralph Ellison termed "the greatest American President for the poor and for the Negroes," legislative programs aimed at ending poverty and increasing economic opportunity had given way to oft-stated concern about "law and order" and "crime in the streets," phrases that many observers interpreted as code words concerning the suppression of black unrest. Other Americans feared that in the attention paid to the problems of minorities and the poor their own concerns were being overlooked. Sometimes forgotten in the tumult of debate was that most polls consistently showed a majority of Americans in favor of the war in Vietnam and even supportive of an escalation of the American presence there. These Americans, sometimes called the "backlash vote" or the "silent majority," were destined to play a crucial role in the 1968 election.

These were not Kennedy's people. "I want to work for all who are not represented. I want to be their president," he told the black civil rights leader Charles Evers. "This is a generous and compassionate country," he said at another time. "That's what I want this country to stand for. Not violence, not lawlessness, but compassion, and love and peace." That conviction was challenged in early April when the black civil rights leader Martin Luther King, Jr., the youngest American to receive the Nobel Peace Prize, was assassinated as he stood on a hotel balcony in Memphis, Tennessee. Across the nation, America's black communities vented their grief in rage and violence. There were riots in 76 cities, resulting in thousands of injuries, 28,000 arrests, and millions of dollars in damages. Kennedy was boarding a flight to a campaign appearance in the black section of Indianapolis, Indiana, when he learned of King's death. Aboard the plane he wept.

Influenced by the philosophy of the Indian leader Mahatma Gandhi, the Reverend Martin Luther King, Jr., advocated nonviolent resistance in the struggle for equal rights for black Americans. King's assassination in May 1968 triggered rioting in cities across the nation and deprived the civil rights movement of its most eloquent spokesperson.

Upon his arrival, it was obvious from the crowd's festive mood that the terrible news had not reached them. Kennedy spoke from the back of a flatbed truck, where he appeared, to one television correspondent, "gaunt and distressed and full of anguish." "I have bad news for you, for all of our fellow citizens, and people who love peace throughout the world, and that is that Martin Luther King was shot and killed tonight," he began. The crowd was stunned into silence. "In this difficult day, in this difficult time for the United States," he continued, "it is perhaps well to ask what kind of nation we are and what direction we want to move in. For those of you who are black — considering the evidence there evidently is that there were white people who were responsible — you can be filled with bitterness,

Robert Kennedy addresses a crowd at the University of Nebraska shortly after announcing his candidacy for president in 1968. The passion Kennedy aroused in audiences and his insistence on campaigning without heavy security worried many of his advisers.

with hatred, and a desire for revenge. We can move in that direction as a country, in great polarization — black people amongst black, white people amongst white, filled with hatred toward one another. Or we can make an effort, as Martin Luther King did, to understand and to comprehend, and to replace that violence, that stain of bloodshed that has spread across our land, with an effort to understand, with compassion and love." He spoke then, for the first time in public, of the anguish he felt when his own brother was assassinated and invoked the ancient Greek tragedian Aeschylus, whom he called his "favorite poet." Kennedy said of Aeschylus, "He wrote: 'In our sleep, pain which cannot forget falls drop by drop upon the heart until, in our own despair, against our will, comes wisdom through the awful grace of God.' " He pled again for an end to the awful divisions in American society, saying what was needed was "love and wisdom, and compassion toward one another, and a feeling of justice toward those who still suffer within our country" and asked that his listeners dedicate themselves "to what the Greeks wrote so many years ago: to tame the savageness of man and make gentle the life of this world." He concluded by asking that those gathered say a prayer "for our country."

In a passionate era no public figure aroused more intense emotion than Robert Kennedy. His brother John had been cool and detached and made a virtue of pragmatism; Robert was intuitive and emotional. Critics called Kennedy a self-aggrandizing, ambitious opportunist; those who knew him best insisted he was shy and compassionate. The *New York Times* columnist James Reston wrote in April 1968 that "the opposition to him is personal, almost chemical, and sometimes borders on the irrational." The conflicting feelings Kennedy created were sometimes evident in the same observer. In 1965 the Pulitzer Prize–winning columnist Murray Kempton lauded Kennedy as "our first politician for the pariahs, our great natural outsider, our lonely reproach, the natural standard held out to all rebels." Three years later, angered by Kennedy's belated entrance into the presidential race, Kempton derided him in print as a coward come "down from the hills to shoot the wounded. . . . In one day, he managed to confirm the worst things his enemies have ever said about him." The influential economist and author John Kenneth Galbraith asked rhetorically, "Could it be that he was the least known public figure of our time?"

Those whom Kennedy said he wished to represent — the poor, blacks, Mexican-Americans, Indians, working-class whites, and others effectively disenfranchised by prejudice and lack of economic opportunity — had no such doubts about him. They recognized his empathy for them as genuine and responded accordingly. The historian Arthur Schlesinger, Jr., regarded Kennedy's compulsion "to be at one with individuals in extreme situations [as] increasingly the key to his politics." He believed this sympathetic identification to be rooted in Kennedy's personal suffering over the death of his brother. Schlesinger wrote: "Dallas [where John Kennedy had been killed]. . . had charged sympathy with almost despairing intensity. His own experience of the waste and cruelty of life gave him access to the sufferings of others. He appeared most surely himself among those whom life had left out." The

> *It was almost a fad to hate him.*
> —JACK NEWFIELD
> Kennedy biographer

novelist Norman Mailer observed the "subtle sadness [that] had come to live in his tone of confidence" and noted that "he had come into that world where people live with the recognition of tragedy, and are so often afraid of happiness." In the commonplace book (a collection of literary quotations and other miscellaneous items) Kennedy kept, he included as the epigraph a passage from the poet John Keats: "None can usurp the height but those to whom the miseries of the world are a misery and will not let them rest."

The passion he inspired in his supporters was extraordinary. The Reverend Channing Phillips, a black community leader in Washington, D.C., said that "Bobby Kennedy had this fantastic ability to communicate hope to some pretty rejected people. No other white man has this same quality." Some found it unlikely that this descendant of one of America's richest and most prominent families would identify so closely with the downtrodden, but the writer Vine Deloria, Jr., an American Indian, believed Kennedy "could move from world to world and never be a stranger anywhere." Deloria felt that Kennedy's empathy for the Indians was so great that he "somehow validated undefined feelings of Indian people which they had been unwilling to admit to themselves. Spiritually, he was an Indian."

This passion was evident on the campaign trail, where adulatory crowds swarmed the candidate, eager to muss his hair, shake his hand, touch him. The crush of admirers was sometimes so great that an aide was forced to kneel next to Kennedy and clutch him around the waist to keep him from being pulled from the convertible he used during motorcades. At night his fingers and palms bled from shaking so many hands. At one stop he was yanked from his automobile, chipping a tooth and cutting his lip. On two separate occasions his shoes were taken from his feet. Cufflinks and buttons were regularly torn from his shirt and suit jacket. The frenzy frightened many, particularly those who had worked and been close with his brother, but Kennedy refused to take extra security precautions.

Scrambling to overcome the disorganized beginnings of the campaign and the opposition of the party leaders, Kennedy won primaries in Indiana and Nebraska. Along the way he challenged those indifferent to or skeptical of his vision of America. When, while trying to convey the horror of urban ghetto life to a gathering of well-heeled Indianapolis businessmen, the group tittered at his assertion that there were more rats than people in New York City, he silenced them with a curt "Don't laugh." When medical students at the University of Indiana asked him where the government would get the funds for his proposed social programs, he reminded them of their privileged positions and said, "From you." At college campuses he reiterated his support for the abolition of the deferments that had allowed college students exemption from service in Vietnam and asked the predominantly white student bodies if they found it fair that in a nation where blacks constituted 11 percent of the population, they made up 45 percent of the fighting forces in Vietnam. In a similar vein he stated his opposition to an amnesty for those who had fled to Canada and other countries to avoid being drafted into the military. Opposition to the war was justified, he believed, but those who felt strongly enough to dissent should be willing to pay the consequences. To indifferent audiences he spoke about

The surging and exultant crowds that greeted this Kennedy motorcade through Detroit, Michigan, in May 1968 were characteristic of his 85-day campaign for the presidency. Ten months earlier the city's black neighborhoods had been the scene of rioting, arson, and looting that required military force to subdue.

the plight of the American Indian, asking them if they did not find it unacceptable, as he did, that "the first American is still the last American in terms of employment, health, and education." Always he closed with a paraphrase of a quote from the Irish dramatist George Bernard Shaw: "Some men see things as they are and say 'Why?' I dream of things that never were and say 'Why not?' "

The Kennedy momentum came to a halt in Oregon, where the predominantly white (nearly 99 percent), prosperous electorate proved unreceptive to his message. McCarthy's victory in the Oregon primary marked the first electoral defeat ever suffered by a member of the Kennedy family and made the upcoming primary in California, the last to be held before the convention, that much more important.

In a state that was regarded as a demographic microcosm of the entire country, Kennedy won 46.3 percent of the popular vote to 41.8 percent for McCarthy. He took 170 of California's 173 delegates, which put him well ahead of McCarthy in the delegate count but still trailing Hubert Humphrey, the vice-president, who had entered the race after Johnson's withdrawal. Enjoying the support of many of the Democratic governors, mayors, and other party leaders who would control large blocs of delegates at the convention, Humphrey had not deemed it necessary to enter the primaries. Still, as Kennedy stepped up to the microphone that June night in Los Angeles, his supporters were optimistic that in the months before the convention the popularity he demonstrated with voters in the primaries would be sufficient to sway enough of the estimated 872 uncommitted delegates to secure him the nomination.

As always, his ginger hair was tousled, and he nervously pushed it back from his forehead. Although he was of average size — 5 feet 10 inches tall, 155 pounds — and was an enthusiastic if not overly skilled athlete, some saw him as slight and fragile. He began on a light note, congratulating Los Angeles Dodgers' pitcher Don Drysdale, who that night had pitched a record sixth straight shutout. Then he thanked his supporters and campaign workers, his wife, Ethel, and his beloved springer spaniel, Freck-

les. Finally, he discussed the meaning of his victory. He said that he thought it "quite clear that we can work together . . . [to end] what has been going on within the United States over a period of the last three years — the division, the violence, the disenchantment with our society; the divisions, whether it's between blacks and whites, between the poor and the more affluent, or between age groups or on the war in Vietnam. . . . We are a great country, an unselfish country, and a compassionate country. I intend to make that my basis for running."

He finished, and his aides led him through the kitchen and pantry area toward a news conference scheduled in a nearby room. It was shortly after midnight. As Kennedy moved down the kitchen corridor past an ice machine, a young man stepped into the hallway, leaned above the senator's aides, and from a distance of only a few feet fired a revolver at the candidate's head. As Kennedy slumped to the floor, aides grabbed the assailant, who continued to fire wildly. Four more people were wounded. Pandemonium spread from the hallway to the Embassy Room, where the horrified crowd learned that Robert Kennedy had been shot.

Hubert Humphrey made a campaign stop at Stevens Point, Wisconsin, on behalf of Johnson on March 23, 1968, eight days before the president announced he would not seek reelection. Many historians believe that Humphrey's refusal to repudiate explicitly Johnson's Vietnam policy cost him the presidential election in November.

2

The Family

There was little in Robert Francis Kennedy's background to suggest that he would become the champion of the poor and underprivileged. He was born in Brookline, Massachusetts, an affluent Boston suburb, on November 20, 1925. His father, Joseph Patrick Kennedy, 37 years old at the time of his seventh child's birth, had already had successful careers in banking, utilities, and shipping and was engaged in the canny speculation that would make him a legendary fortune on the stock market. The son of a first-generation Irish American whose hard work and political connections had enabled him to rise from saloonkeeper to bank president, the Harvard-educated Joseph Kennedy railed against the barriers that Protestants in Boston had erected to preserve their privileged enclaves.

The Irish first came to Boston (and other locations in the United States) in great numbers in the 1840s, after the failure of the potato crop in Ireland resulted in horrible famine there. The predominantly Roman Catholic newcomers met with widespread discrimination from Boston's white Anglo-Saxon Protestant elite, who stereotyped them as rowdy drunkards enslaved by a superstitious religion, particularly after

He is just starting off and he has the difficulty of trying to follow two brilliant brothers, Joe and Jack. That in itself is quite a handicap and he is making good progress against it.
—JOSEPH KENNEDY, SR.
1948

Kennedy's parents, Joseph and Rose, in 1928. Joseph Kennedy's fierce desire to succeed was fired by resentment against the class and social barriers that still existed for Irish Americans in Boston. He accumulated a massive fortune as an investment banker, stock speculator, and movie producer.

The Kennedy family in 1934. Front row, left to right: Patricia, Rose, Edward, Joseph, Sr., Kathleen, Eunice, and Rosemary. Back row, from left: John, Jeanne, and nine-year-old Robert. Joseph, Jr., is not shown.

the Irish demonstrated an aptitude for electoral politics that soon enabled them to control many levels of city government. The Protestant elite responded by establishing a system of private schools and social organizations that enabled the more prestigious families to cement the class and family ties that allowed them to dominate the economic life of the city. The No Irish Need Apply signs that were a not uncommon sight in Boston galled Joseph Kennedy, as did his exclusion from the more prestigious clubs and societies at Harvard. He was determined that no such barriers would exist for his children.

Robert's mother, Rose Fitzgerald Kennedy, was the daughter of a colorful politician, John Francis Fitzgerald. Known as Honey Fitz for the "honey-sweet voice" with which he crooned his theme song, "Sweet Adeline," at political rallies, Fitzgerald served several terms as mayor of Boston and as a U.S. congressman. Born in 1890, Rose grew up in the privileged world that Boston's prosperous Irish Catholics had created in response to their exclusion from Protestant social circles. Where the Kennedys wished to knock down any remaining barriers to assimilation, families such as the Fitzgeralds were content with political power and creating their own counterparts to Boston's high society. Rose was educated in convents in Boston, New York, and the Netherlands and vacationed in Maine and Florida. While in Europe she became fluent in French and German. At 21 she was given a lavish coming-out party by her father. At about the same time she fell in love with Joseph Kennedy. Against her father's wishes — Honey Fitz and Patrick Kennedy had a long-standing distaste for one another — the two married in October 1914.

Joseph Kennedy placed his family above all things, including business. "The measure of a man's success," he said, "is not the money he's made. It's the kind of family he has raised." His children were raised to be competitive and tough, giving rise to the family maxim "Kennedys don't cry." The children were encouraged to compete with each other in everything, be it athletics or academics, with their father's approval the greatest prize. To Joseph Kennedy, losing was only slightly less unforgivable than not giving one's all. The rivalry between the two oldest boys, Joseph, Jr., and John, was particularly fierce. The older and more athletic Joe, Jr., usually won the fights, while the sickly and bookish John could often outwit his older brother in argument. By all accounts the most sensitive and shy of the Kennedy children, young Robert — Bobby to family and friends — remembered "cowering with his sisters upstairs while his older brothers fought furiously on the first floor."

Bobby was more like his father and Jack was more like his mother. . . . Bobby was more direct, dynamic, energizing; Jack was more thoughtful, more scholarly, more reflective.
—WILLIAM O. DOUGLAS
former Supreme
Court justice

A concerned crowd waits outside the New York Stock Exchange during the stock market crash of October 1929. Joseph Kennedy removed his investments from the market before the crash and later became one of the most prominent businessmen to support President Franklin Roosevelt's plans for reforming and rebuilding the economy during the Great Depression.

When Bobby was four his father moved the family from Boston, first to Riverdale and then to Bronxville, then wealthy suburbs of New York City. The family always maintained that Joseph moved because he was tired of Boston's anti-Irish prejudice, but others have speculated that there was more money to be made in New York. The family also maintained homes along Millionaires' Row in Palm Beach, Florida, and in Hyannis Port, Massachusetts.

Ever the shrewd speculator, Joseph Kennedy was among the fortunate few who got their money out of the stock market before it crashed in October 1929. The depression that followed the stock market crash demolished the U.S. economy and resulted in unparalleled unemployment and economic hardship. An enthusiastic and generous supporter of Franklin Roosevelt, who was elected president in 1932, Kennedy lambasted businessmen for the shortsightedness and greed that many believed had helped cause the Great Depression. While much of the business community raged against the economic regulation that formed an integral part of Roosevelt's New Deal legislation, Kennedy actively sought a position within the administration and in 1934 was named the first chairman of the Securities and Exchange Commission, a new agency created to oversee the stock market.

The New Deal and current events dominated dinnertime conversation at the Kennedy home. Only serious subjects were suitable topics for discussion at these mealtime forums. Joseph Kennedy encouraged his children to question him on politics, economics, and history. The children, in turn, were expected to be prepared to respond to their father's inquiries. As an adult Robert Kennedy wrote, "I can hardly remember a mealtime when the conversation was not dominated by what Franklin D. Roosevelt was doing or what was happening in the world." Disagreement was frequent and encouraged, and vociferous argument was not uncommon. Kennedy fully expected his children's political viewpoints and interpretations to differ from his own. Any opinion was acceptable, provided its holder could make an articulate and reasoned defense of it. The only forbidden subject was business, with which Joseph Kennedy now professed a certain boredom. He believed that after the depression, government, not business, would be the place for the young and ambitious to make their mark. Kennedy believed that the increased governmental regulation of the economy characteristic of the New Deal was a harbinger of a new age in which the federal government would

Bobby (right) and his younger brother, Teddy, were photographed at the opening of London's children's zoo in 1938. The Kennedy children became popular subject matter for British newspapers when they joined their father, who was serving as U.S. ambassador to Great Britain, in London in 1938.

play a larger role in virtually every area of American life. "In the next generation," Kennedy said in the 1930s, "the people who run the government will be the biggest people in America." Accordingly, the boys were groomed for public service from a young age. Kennedy told his wife, "The boys might as well work for the government, because politics will control the business of the country in the future."

As the shiest and least vocal of the Kennedy children, Bobby was usually overshadowed by his older brothers during dinnertime conversation, but he had inherited the Kennedy drive. A poor natural athlete, as a very young boy he dove off a sailboat in order to teach himself to swim and had to be fished from the water by his brother Joe. The one area where he did not give his all was academics. In grade school he was an adequate but undistinguished student. He later told the journalist Jack Newfield that what he remembered about his early years was "going to a lot of different schools, always having to make new friends, and that I was very awkward. I dropped things and fell down all the time. I had to go to the hospital a few times for stitches in my head and leg. And I was pretty quiet most of the time. And I didn't mind being alone."

There is little doubt that Joseph Kennedy, Jr., shown here in the early 1930s as a member of Harvard University's freshman football team, was his parents' favorite. His death during a World War II flying mission devastated his parents, particularly his father, who had been grooming his oldest son for a political career.

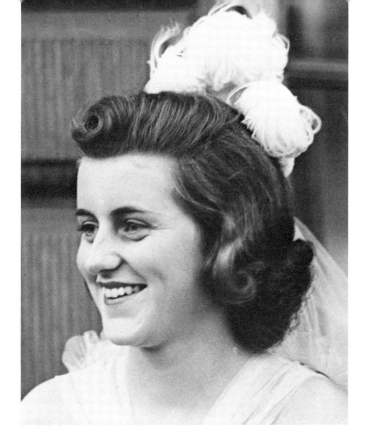

The outgoing personality of the oldest Kennedy girl, Kathleen, captivated the British during her time in England. She is shown here on her way to a ball at Buckingham Palace in 1938. As a Red Cross volunteer in England during World War II, she met William Hartington Cavendish, a member of the British nobility, and the two were eventually married.

He observed to another writer that "I was the seventh of nine children, and when you come from that far down you have to struggle to survive."

Joseph Kennedy's work in the Roosevelt administration — he was appointed head of the Maritime Commission in 1937 and ambassador to Great Britain later that same year — kept him away from home frequently, and Bobby became particularly close to his mother. Like their father, his older brothers observed the outward rituals of Catholicism without possessing any great degree of inward commitment, but from an early age Bobby was a devout Catholic. While the pious Rose advocated a Catholic education for her children, Joseph decreed that his sons would be sent to preparatory boarding schools and then to Harvard University. (The Kennedy daughters received a Catholic education.) At the age of 13 Bobby was sent to the prestigious St. Paul's Academy in Concord, New Hampshire, but his complaints that he was forced to attend Protestant religious services there found his mother a sympathetic listener. With his father away in London,

Bobby was enrolled in Portsmouth Priory, a Catholic institution near Newport, Rhode Island, run by Benedictine monks. There he attended mass three times a week as well as Sunday, often served as an altar boy, and took part in twice-daily prayer services. He continued to be an indifferent student, however, making his worst grades, surprisingly, in history and Christian doctrine.

Deeming his academic progress unsatisfactory, his father removed Bobby from Portsmouth and enrolled him in the Milton Academy, in Milton, Massachusetts, in the fall of 1942. It was hard for a shy new boy to gain social acceptance at Milton, but his way was made easier by his friendship with David Hackett, Milton's most outstanding athlete. The model for Phineas, the golden hero of the writer John Knowles's novel *A Separate Peace*, Hackett admired Kennedy's earnestness and dogged determination to do the right thing, even at the expense of acceptance by his peers. Hackett told Arthur Schlesinger, Jr., that Kennedy was "neither a natural athlete nor a natural student nor a natural success with girls and had no natural gift for popularity. Nothing came easily for him. What he had was a set of handicaps and a fantastic determination to overcome them. The handicaps made him redouble his effort." His teachers praised his seriousness of mind, sense of humor, religious conviction, and concern for others.

In the meantime the United States had entered World War II. Although Joseph Kennedy was vehemently opposed to U.S. involvement under any circumstances — a viewpoint that led to his resignation as ambassador and a permanent rift with Roosevelt — his two oldest sons were both already enlisted in the navy at the time of the Japanese attack on Pearl Harbor on December 7, 1941. Joe, Jr., volunteered for flight training, while John received training for service on PT (patrol torpedo) boats. PTs were fast, extremely maneuverable motorboats, 60 to 100 feet in length, equipped with machine guns, torpedoes, and depth charges. By spring 1943 John was in command of his own boat, PT 109, stationed in the Solomon Islands in the western Pacific. On the night of August 1, a group of PT boats engaged four Japanese destroyers in combat. In the heat of battle PT 109 was run over and cut in half by one of the Japanese destroyers. Kennedy led the 11 surviving crew members (one man was lost) to safety on a nearby atoll (coral reef), towing one badly burned sailor himself. For the next several days he swam back and forth between nearby islands, hoping to contact a PT patrol, but rescue did not come until the survivors were discovered by some islanders, who were dispatched to the American installation on the island of Rendova with an SOS message Kennedy carved into a coconut shell.

John Kennedy's heroism was front-page news in the United States, but the next exploit of Kennedy bravery was not to end so fortunately. Joe Kennedy, Jr., had already completed two tours of duty by the time of the D-Day invasion of France in June 1944, but he extended his tour so as to be present for the invasion. Two months later he volunteered for an extremely dangerous mission, piloting a plane laden with explosives toward a giant concrete bunker near the French seaport of Calais believed to be the launching site for the V-1 rockets the Germans were

Seventeen-year-old Bobby Kennedy is sworn in as a naval cadet in October 1943 as his father looks on. The wartime heroism of his two older brothers left the competitive Robert eager to see action, but he was still stateside when World War II came to an end in August 1945.

using with such deadly effectiveness against the civilian population of London. At a certain point Kennedy and his copilot were to parachute from their aircraft, which would then be guided by remote control into the bunker. The flight took place on August 12. Twenty-six minutes into the mission, Kennedy's plane exploded. The pilot of an accompanying plane said "it was the biggest explosion I ever saw until pictures of the atom bomb." Its force damaged 59 buildings below in the tiny English village of Newdelight Woods.

Handsome and vital, Joe, Jr., had been his parents' favorite child. Most of his father's hopes for the future were invested in young Joe, who had been groomed for a political career. Whereas Rose was able to find consolation for her loss in Catholicism, the elder Joseph Kennedy was inconsolable. Even years later the mention of his oldest son sometimes reduced him to tears.

Like his brothers, Bobby had been eager to join the service and go to war. While finishing up at Milton in October 1943, Bobby had enlisted as an apprentice seaman in the Naval Reserve. Five months later he was in officers' training at Harvard. His brother's death left Bobby's desire for active duty undiminished, but he would remain stateside until war's end. Leaving his officers' training unfinished, he completed his military duty in May 1946 by serving as a seaman aboard the newly commissioned destroyer the *Joseph P. Kennedy, Jr.* for its shakedown voyage.

With the death of his oldest son, Joseph Kennedy's political ambitions were transferred to John. Bobby was honorably discharged from the navy in time to assist his brother with his campaign for the U.S. House of Representatives. Military service and family tragedy had given Bobby's character a veneer of toughness. Casual acquaintances were now more likely to see competitiveness and aggression than the gentleness and sensitivity that had been evident in his earlier years. He now seemed fully to ascribe to the Kennedy belief that it was weakness to display one's emotions except through humor, and his was usually deemed cutting and sarcastic. The change

With the death of his older brother, John Kennedy became the object of his father's political ambition for his sons. He was first elected to the U.S. House of Representatives in 1946 and is shown here shortly after his 1952 election to the Senate. Robert Kennedy's expert management of his brother's senatorial campaign helped foster a growing closeness between the two.

was in large part due to the continued need to prove himself to his father and older brother. Although Joseph Kennedy now paid more attention to his third son, Bobby was still regarded as too inexperienced to play a crucial role in the campaign and was assigned responsibility for three wards in which Kennedy's opponent was particularly strong. Bobby campaigned tirelessly, launching the stories of his ruthlessness by evicting from campaign headquarters some old political cronies of Honey Fitz's whom he believed were freeloading. John won the party primary (and subsequent election to Congress), and although he lost in each of Bobby's wards, the margin of defeat was much smaller than expected.

Bobby enrolled at Harvard, as his brothers had done before him, in September. He was given academic credit for his officers' training and entered the university as a junior. Although his knowledge of politics and current affairs impressed those who knew him, he was again an indifferent student. A government major, he received average grades and went unnoticed by his professors. His main interest was football, where as an undersized end his play was characterized by determination and aggressiveness rather than skill. Another member of the Harvard football squad remembered that Kennedy "had no right to make the squad. He didn't have much speed and he didn't have any special moves. But he practiced harder than anyone else, and if he got knocked down he got up and came at you harder than before." By his senior year he was a starter and even scored a touchdown in the team's first game, but he broke his leg in practice a few days later. Although he tried to keep the fracture a secret and kept on playing until he collapsed, the injury ended his season, except for a few plays — with his leg still in a cast — against traditional rival Yale in the season finale. Nevertheless, he earned a varsity letter, an achievement that had eluded his brothers. He was also the first Kennedy to collect the $2,000 Joseph, Sr., had offered to any of his sons who refrained from smoking or drinking until their 21st birthday.

After graduating from Harvard with a bachelor's degree in March 1948, Kennedy left almost immediately on a grand tour of Europe and the Middle East. Seeing the trip as an opportunity for his son to gain practical experience and learn about foreign affairs, Joseph Kennedy arranged for Bobby to be accredited as a correspondent for the *Boston Post*. He visited England, Egypt, Palestine, Lebanon, Turkey, Greece, Italy, Belgium, Holland, West Germany and West Berlin, Austria, Denmark, and Ireland. His most insightful dispatches came from Palestine and spoke of the failure of British policy there, the hatred of both the Arabs and Jews for the British, and the inevitability of war in the Middle East. While he was abroad his older sister Kathleen (five years his senior) was killed in a plane crash. Four years earlier Kathleen had stunned her family by marrying William Hartington Cavendish, an English nobleman who was the son of the duke of Devonshire. Cavendish's family was a pillar of the Church of England, and Rose had been distraught at the thought of her daughter marrying outside the Catholic church. Both Joseph, Sr., and Joseph, Jr., had supported Kathleen in her decision. Mother and daughter had reconciled after Cavendish's death in September 1944, although friction had newly developed over Kathleen's romance with a twice-divorced Englishman. Bedridden with jaundice in Italy, Bobby was unable to attend the funeral.

Although Joseph Kennedy's fortune ensured that none of his children would have to work for a living — each was provided with a trust fund that, in the words of their father, enabled "any of my children, financially speaking, [to] look me in the eye and tell me to go to hell" — the boys were expected to have careers, preferably in politics. Bobby decided on law school. His grades were insufficient for admission to Harvard, but he was admitted, with reservations, to the law school at the University of Virginia. The admissions committee there commented that "unless he does better work than he did at Harvard, he is unlikely to succeed in this law school."

Bobby succeeded but did not distinguish himself. He graduated in June 1951 with a 2.54 grade point

Robert Kennedy married Ethel Skakel in Greenwich, Connecticut, in June 1950. She shared his love for sports, and her spontaneous good humor helped lighten his moodiness. In their 18 years of what was by all accounts a happy marriage, they had 11 children.

average (out of a possible 4.0), which ranked him 56th in a class of 124. His professors believed that he did not work overly hard at his studies because natural ability enabled him to succeed with little effort. The most important event of his three years at law school was his courtship of Ethel Skakel, the athletic and vivacious daughter of a wealthy midwestern minerals and shipping magnate. He had first met Ethel in 1946, when his sister Jean brought her home on a vacation from college to help with John's campaign. Like Bobby, Ethel was a younger child — the sixth of seven — in a large Catholic family. The outgoing and informal Ethel helped relax the shy and serious Bobby, and the two were married in June 1950. Their first child, Kathleen Hartington Kennedy, was born 13 months later, a month after Bobby's law school graduation. The young couple soon set up house in the Georgetown section of Washington, D.C., where Bobby — the first of the Kennedys to enter a profession — had taken a job with the U.S. Justice Department.

3

Building a Reputation

Kennedy was happy in Washington and with his work for the Justice Department, but when John asked him to return to Massachusetts to run his senatorial campaign, family loyalty prevailed. John's opponent for the seat was the extremely popular incumbent, Henry Cabot Lodge, Jr., the scion of one of Boston's first families. When Robert came on board the campaign was in disarray, caused mainly by Joseph Kennedy's insistence on running affairs. In the eyes of John's younger staffers — most of whom were World War II veterans — the elder Kennedy was directing the campaign based on an outdated concept of Massachusetts politics dating back to the days of the great Irish-American ward bosses and political machines, a time when large blocs of votes were exchanged for patronage jobs, contracts, and other favors. Although such practices were by no means extinct, the young aides around John Kennedy were comfortable with a newer-style politics in which issues, not loyalty and jobs, were the most important factors in winning votes. Kenneth O'Donnell, a close personal friend of the two Kennedy brothers, complained that Joseph surrounded

> *In 1952, [during John Kennedy's Senate campaign] Bobby told party luminaries hanging around headquarters to lick envelopes or get out.*
> —TOM MATHEWS
> American journalist

Robert Kennedy with one of his seven sons. Kennedy delighted in the vitality and unpredictability his 11 children and their innumerable pets lent life at Hickory Hill, the family home in McLean, Virginia.

41

John with "elder statesmen who knew nothing about the politics in this day and age, and he assumed, despite the fact that he had not been in Massachusetts for 20 years, that it was the same thing . . . and he's such a strong personality that nobody could—nobody dared—fight back."

Robert immediately took charge of the campaign. He was unconcerned about offending the politicians whom his father had so assiduously courted. "Politicians do nothing but hold meetings," he said. "You can't get any work out of a politician." From the 1952 senatorial campaign was born the legend of the "Kennedy machine," said to be a sleek, streamlined political juggernaut characterized by brilliant planning and infallible organization and fueled by Joseph Kennedy's millions. Overseeing all was Robert Kennedy. As would be the pattern in future elections and crises, Robert was the one John expected to carry out the onerous but necessary tasks considered impolitic for the candidate to perform himself. When Paul Dever, the incumbent Democratic governor, fell behind in his bid for re-election, he sought an alliance with the Kennedy campaign. Not wishing to be tied too closely to the faltering Dever effort, John instructed his brother to tell Dever that it would be impossible for the two campaigns to merge, but to make this known in such a way that it would appear the rebuff was Robert's idea, not John's. "Don't give in to them," Robert was instructed by his brother, "but don't get me involved in it. Treat it as an organizational matter." Robert's blunt refusal so enraged Dever that he ordered that "kid" to be kept out of his office, but his animosity was directed at Robert, not the Kennedy campaign, and he continued to support John's senatorial bid.

Handsome, wealthy, Irish Catholic (in a state with a large Irish-Catholic constituency), war hero, and author of a best-selling book — *Why England Slept*, a study of Britain's unpreparedness at the outbreak of World War II — John Kennedy was an extremely attractive candidate. Still, much of the credit for his election to the U.S. Senate was due his younger brother. Kenneth O'Donnell said, "Bobby could han-

dle the father, and no one else could have. . . . Those of us who worked with him over the last few months are convinced that if Bobby had not arrived on the scene and taken charge when he did, Jack Kennedy most certainly would have lost the election." Despite being forced to defer somewhat to the younger generation, Joseph Kennedy was also instrumental in John's election, particularly in securing for his son the endorsement of the Boston *Post*, at that time a newspaper with a conservative, Republican-oriented editorial bent whose imprimatur Lodge deemed equal to 40,000 votes. The *Post's* endorsement was followed by a $500,000 loan from Joseph Kennedy to its financially beleaguered publisher, John Fox.

Robert's work on the campaign brought him the praise and admiration of his father and brought the two brothers closer together. The qualities that contributed to charges of ruthlessness earned his father's respect. "He's hard as nails," Joseph proudly said to a reporter about Robert. Joseph believed that Robert could be counted on to maintain the family solidarity that was a source of such pride to the father. He told a journalist in 1957 that "Bobby's a tough one. He'll keep the Kennedys together, you can bet."

John Kennedy arrives at campaign headquarters in Boston, Massachusetts, shortly after learning that he had defeated Henry Cabot Lodge, Jr., in the senatorial election of 1952. Robert Kennedy managed his brother's campaign, and some of the new senator's aides believed his victory would have been impossible without Robert's expert advice.

The two brothers were quite unalike in temperament and personality, and to that point the difference in their ages had kept them from spending much time together. John was more reflective, scholarly, and thoughtful and more independent in his relationship to his family and his faith than Robert was. Emotional and intuitive, Robert was more direct and inclined to judge in terms of right and wrong. He lacked the outward sophistication and charm of his brother John, although those who got to know him were disarmed by his self-deprecatory humor and described him as a warm and complex individual. His friendships were characterized by deep loyalty on both sides. Whereas John was an inveterate womanizer whose prowling would continue even after marriage, Robert was a family man. He and Ethel had their second child, Joseph Patrick III, in 1952, and by the end of the decade they would have four more children. Some who knew him regarded Robert as a "Puritan," and dinner guests at Robert and Ethel's Washington home were amused to learn that the couple kept no alcoholic beverages or ashtrays in the house. Even so, politics formed a common ground for a relationship that would grow increasingly close with the years.

Kennedy huddles with Joseph McCarthy in 1954, shortly after the Wisconsin senator was censured by his colleagues for irresponsible tactics in investigating alleged domestic subversion. Kennedy's association with McCarthy was often cited by critics as an example of his insensitivity to civil liberties issues.

John respected his brother's immense abilities, and in a world in which advice, alliances, and even friendships were based on expediency he looked to Robert as the one person he could absolutely trust. With his great capacity for loyalty and devotion to a cause, Robert readily committed himself to his brother's political career.

With John elected, it was time for Robert to resume his own life. He had resigned from the Justice Department to manage his brother's campaign, so his father made a phone call to Joseph McCarthy, Republican senator from Wisconsin, to ask if he would appoint his son chief counsel. McCarthy was a rough and charming Irishman who had briefly dated two of the Kennedy daughters. He was a particular favorite of Joseph Kennedy and had made several visits to the family home at Hyannis Port.

McCarthy had a mania for publicity, and he had seized upon an inflammatory issue with which to capture the public's attention. After World War II the United States and the Soviet Union entered into an economic and political rivalry known as the cold war. Cold war theory saw communism (the economic and political system based on common ownership of property) as the enemy of both democracy and capitalism (the economic system based on competitive enterprise and private ownership) in a global struggle for the hearts and minds of the people of the world. At home the cold war manifested itself in an obsession with the dangers of communist infiltration of the U.S. government, armed forces, entertainment industry, print media, and the educational system. Fear of domestic subversion was exacerbated by debate over who had "lost" China (where the American-backed government of Chiang Kai-shek was overthrown by a communist regime in 1949), the denunciation of State Department official Alger Hiss as a communist spy, the conviction of Ethel and Julius Rosenberg for selling nuclear secrets to the Soviet Union, that nation's subsequent development of atomic weapons, and U.S. involvement in the war between communist North Korea and South Korea. McCarthy's method was to use sensational but unfounded declarations,

He's the only one who doesn't stick knives in my back, the only one I can count on when it comes down to it.
—JOHN KENNEDY
on Robert Kennedy during
his Senatorial campaign

rumors, and innuendo to capitalize on the widespread fear of communist infiltration of the United States. He began his crusade in February 1950 with a speech in which he asserted that he possessed a list with the names of "a lot" of communists still active in the State Department. This opening salvo was characteristic of the entire McCarthy crusade. Although a Senate commission appointed to investigate the charges concluded that McCarthy had worked a "fraud and a hoax," he had touched a nerve. McCarthy possessed a keen instinct for playing on the emotions of an already fearful public — the journalist Richard Rovere said that no politician had a "surer, swifter access to the dark places of the American mind" — and was a master manipulator of the mass media, which he recognized was obligated to report all of his allegations as he made them. More grandiose and similarly unsubstantiated charges followed. In the climate of hysteria that ensued, mere membership in or even sympathy with various organizations at any point in a person's life, without evidence of past or present disloyalty, was enough to cause one to be subpoenaed by a congressional committee or dismissed from his or her job. Unfounded allegations of past political affiliations or "suspicious" personal associations and tastes in reading material served as sufficient grounds for an individual to be blacklisted, or prevented from working in his or her chosen field. Writers, foreign service officers, actors, teachers and educators, military officers, and many other individuals had their careers and reputations damaged, in many cases irreparably.

When McCarthy received Joseph Kennedy's phone call he was riding high as chairman of the Senate's Permanent Subcommittee on Investigations of the Government Operations Committee. He had already selected his chief counsel, a 25-year-old New York attorney named Roy Cohn who had assisted in the prosecution of the Rosenbergs. Kennedy took a position as assistant counsel. His first assignment was researching trade by U.S. allies with Communist China, which was opposing the

United States in the war in Korea, and the failure of the State Department in putting an end to such commerce. The report he issued after six months was well documented, made no unfounded assertions, and did not imply that the State Department's policy was a result of disloyalty. Shortly after its submission, Kennedy resigned. With Cohn on his staff McCarthy had become even more irresponsible. Kennedy said later that his work under McCarthy grew out of his concern with what he felt to be a legitimate issue — domestic subversion — but that he simply could not abide McCarthy's tactics. Nevertheless, his failure to disavow McCarthy more explicitly would haunt him in the future.

Kennedy's solid work had caught the attention of the three Democratic members of the Subcommittee on Investigations — Stuart Symington of Missouri, John McClellan of Arkansas, Henry Jackson of Washington — who asked him in January 1954 to return as minority counsel. McCarthy and his aides had grown more reckless. Cohn and his personal assistant, G. David Schine, had gone on a highly publicized tour of American embassies in Europe, where they ordered scores of books on embassy shelves burned as subversive literature.

Kennedy became chief counsel for a Senate committee investigating labor racketeering in 1956. The group was chaired by Senator John McClellan of Arkansas (far left). Other members included Senator Karl Mundt of Indiana (far right) and McCarthy (right).

Kennedy's most controversial work with the Rackets Committee was his investigation of the powerful Teamsters union. Kennedy (shown flanked by McClellan and his brother John) uncovered a host of financial irregularities on the part of the labor organization's president, Dave Beck, and his relatives.

McCarthy now claimed that the army was a hotbed of subversion, allegations Cohn encouraged after Schine was drafted. During the televised McCarthy-Army hearings Kennedy assisted the three Democratic senators in their attempts to undermine McCarthy and Cohn. His efforts were so successful that an enraged Cohn took a punch at him during one recess.

The Army hearings proved to be McCarthy's undoing. Television enabled the public to witness firsthand McCarthy's bullying and outrageous tactics. Most viewers were not amused by his questioning the loyalty of generals and other career officers. Revelations of the pressure Cohn had brought to bear on the military in order to void Schine's conscription also helped turn public sentiment against McCarthy. Alert to the shift in opinion, the Senate voted in December 1954 to censure McCarthy. His power gone, the senator from Wisconsin sank into an alcoholic decline, which culminated in his death 29 months later. (One of his last visitors was Robert Kennedy.) Kennedy's reaction to McCarthy's censure was complex: Although he supported it from a political standpoint, he was unable to forget his personal affection for McCarthy and felt sorrow at his ruin. His brother John, perhaps out of reluctance to offend Massachusetts's Irish-Catholic voters, among whom McCarthy was popular, had been the sole Democratic senator not to vote for censure.

The off-year elections of November 1954 returned a Democratic majority to the Senate, and McClellan replaced McCarthy as chairman of the Subcommittee on Investigations. Kennedy became majority counsel. The committee now did its work in more solid, if much less spectacular, fashion, focusing on corruption and mismanagement in the awarding of government contracts. Kennedy continued to make a name for himself as a tireless researcher and dogged cross-examiner. He took time out from his work in the summer of 1955 to tour the Soviet Union with Supreme Court Justice William O. Douglas, a close friend of his father's, and again the following summer, when he served as a delegate from Massachusetts to the Democratic National Convention in Chicago.

As he had been in 1952, Adlai Stevenson was the Democrats' choice for president in 1956. Unable to decide on a running mate, the liberal former governor of Illinois left the choice to the party's delegates. Coming into the convention, John Kennedy's name had been bandied about as an attractive choice for vice-president. Convinced that Stevenson would be soundly defeated, Joseph Kennedy advised his son not to seek the nomination, but when the selection was thrown open to the floor John decided

Critics charged that the Rackets Committee's prolonged investigation of Teamsters executive Jimmy Hoffa (right), who was accused of embezzlement, fraud, coercion, and organized crime connections, was the result of a personal vendetta on the part of Robert Kennedy, who, after he became attorney general, continued to pursue Hoffa.

Campaign manager Robert Kennedy with fellow supporters of his brother's 1960 bid for the presidency. John Kennedy soundly defeated his major challenger in the primaries, Senator Hubert Humphrey, helping to dispel criticism that his youth and religion presented insurmountable obstacles to his election.

to seek the position. Robert was pressed into service to manage the floor fight for the nomination. For the next 12 hours he ran from the floor to hotel suites, trying to call in favors and make deals that would gather enough delegates to secure his brother's nomination. Unprepared and inexperienced, he made several mistakes. The Kennedy movement fell short — Senator Estes Kefauver of Tennessee was the delegation's choice — but in the process Robert Kennedy picked up valuable information about the inner workings of the nominating process.

Kennedy's education in national politics continued when he signed on as an adviser to Stevenson's presidential campaign. Widely considered the most articulate spokesman of liberal Democratic philosophy, Stevenson was very popular among highly educated voters, but he had been soundly defeated in 1952 by the Republican candidate, the even more popular hero of World War II, Dwight Eisenhower. An enthusiastic Stevenson supporter in 1952, Kennedy discovered that close exposure to the candidate on the campaign trail led to severe disillusionment. Kennedy was appalled by the campaign's disorganization, which he found reflective of Stevenson's inability to make a decision, and watched in horror as manpower and resources were misused and valuable hours frittered away in inconclusive campaign meetings on questions that he believed should have been decided in minutes. Convinced that Stevenson was unqualified for executive leadership, Kennedy voted for Eisenhower in the November election, but his experience had been a valuable one. He came away from the Stevenson debacle — Eisenhower was again the overwhelming winner — certain that he knew how a national campaign should be run and even more certain that he knew what ought not to be done. The prize-winning journalist Harrison Salisbury, who covered the Stevenson campaign, wrote of Robert Kennedy: "What surprised me about him at that time, in spite of his great youth and seeming detachment from what was going on, was his great analytical ability. . . . I had the feeling after the Stevenson campaign that Bobby knew every single thing there was to know about a campaign."

He returned to his work in the Senate, this time as chief counsel of a special select committee on Improper Activities in the Labor or Management Field chaired by John McClellan. The group, soon to be popularly known as the Rackets Committee, was composed of four members apiece from the permanent Investigations and Labor committees, evenly divided between Democrats and Republicans. One of its members was John Kennedy.

In the 1930s, New Deal legislation had guaranteed America's workers the right to form unions, giving them the power of collective bargaining. The late 1930s and 1940s saw the development of huge trade unions. These sophisticated labor organizations concerned themselves not only with securing higher wages for their members but with providing pensions and accident, disability, and strike insurance. As Kennedy began his research, he became aware of numerous allegations that union executives were using pension and welfare funds for their own personal enrichment. Even more disturbing were reports that organized crime figures had muscled their way into positions of power in several unions, drawn by the money to be siphoned from union treasuries and the opportunities for shakedowns

I've seen a lot of counsels here. There was no one like him. He had an uncanny ability to get people to do more than they thought they could do.

—LAVERN DUFFY an investigator with the Rackets Committee, on Kennedy's performance as chief counsel

Kennedy on the floor of the 1960 Democratic convention, held in Los Angeles, California, where his organizational abilities enabled his brother to secure the nomination for president by staving off last-minute challenges from Adlai Stevenson and Lyndon Johnson.

and extortion that control of a large body of organized laborers made possible.

The most serious charges concerned the International Brotherhood of Teamsters (a giant union composed primarily of truck drivers), its president, David Beck, and one of its top executives, Jimmy Hoffa. Kennedy communicated with numerous union members who told him that Teamsters officials had rigged union elections, embezzled and stolen from union funds, beaten up and intimidated union members, allowed organized crime figures to infiltrate the union, and profited from the formation of phony local chapters. Reluctant to anger working-class constituents, many senators (including initially John Kennedy) had misgivings about an investigation that could be construed as antilabor, but Robert Kennedy saw things differently, believing that it was the Racket Committee's duty to protect union members who had been betrayed by their leadership, had their pension funds stolen, or been denied proper representation because of fraudulent elections. From Kennedy's point of view, organizations designed to protect the interests of the working class had been corrupted from within and essentially handed over to criminal elements. Those whom the unions were supposed to protect no longer had much say in how they were run.

The investigation focused first on Beck. Using newspaper reports, the testimony of witnesses, and the aid of expert accountants, Kennedy and his assistants uncovered a trail of financial chicanery and malfeasance (misconduct) that led them, in Kennedy's words, to "the startling but inescapable conclusion that Dave Beck, the president of America's largest and most powerful union . . . was a crook." Testimony before the McClellan subcommittee laid the groundwork for Beck's subsequent conviction for larceny and income tax evasion. Many applauded Kennedy's work. George Meany, head of the AFL-CIO (the American Federation of Labor and Congress of Industrial Organizations, a giant alliance

John Kennedy and his opponent in the 1960 presidential election, Richard M. Nixon, shortly before their first nationally televised debate. Most viewers felt that Kennedy came across as more knowledgeable and poised than the older and more experienced Nixon.

of trade unions), pledged cooperation with the subcommittee and observed that Beck's was the case of a "very, very wealthy individual spending every waking moment . . . to find some way to use his union as an instrumentality for his own profit." The AFL-CIO expelled the Teamsters. Still, Kennedy's revelations were not universally popular. Beck had done much to make the Teamsters a powerful union, and he numbered many prominent politicians and businessmen among his admirers.

Kennedy next turned his tireless energy and that of his staff to Hoffa, who succeeded Beck as the Teamsters' president. Kennedy obtained testimonials from Teamsters members and other evidence that linked Hoffa to beatings and murders, rigged elections, misuse of funds, the payment and acceptance of bribes, the use of gangsters to enforce his domination of the union, and tampering with the judicial system. When Kennedy cross-examined Hoffa, the contrast between the wiry, boyish prosecutor and the burly trucker and union leader was heightened by the hatred each man held for the other. Hoffa saw Kennedy as a spoiled rich kid who had never had to work a day in his life and possessed no knowledge of the realities of working-class life. To Kennedy, Hoffa was the worst kind of villain, an individual who cynically exploited the loyalty of those who trusted him for his own personal enrichment. Shortly after Hoffa appeared before the Senate subcommittee for the first time, in March 1957, he was arrested and charged with bribery and conspiracy, but a jury acquitted him in July. Kennedy questioned him again in August, this time on his connections with mobsters, but Hoffa was subsequently acquitted of a wiretapping charge and had a perjury indictment dismissed. Kennedy took another crack at him in July 1958, but again no charges stuck.

His cross-examinations of Hoffa made Kennedy a national figure, but they also aroused considerable controversy. Hoffa had many supporters among the Teamsters who praised him for his success in raising wages, reducing working hours, improving conditions, stabilizing labor relations, and ending segregation within the union. Critics found Kennedy brusque, accusatory, and self-righteous, fueled by an excess of misplaced zeal. They interpreted the continuing investigations of Hoffa as a personal vendetta on the part of the chief counsel. It was said that Kennedy was a bully who used public hearings for the "purpose of accusing, judging, and condemning people." Kennedy's grandiose statements — he called a proposed merger of the Teamsters and the longshoremen's union an "unholy alliance that could dominate the United States within three to five years" and termed the Teamsters a "conspiracy of evil" — did nothing to dispel this image, and his willingness to imply criminal motivation to Hoffa's taking the Fifth Amendment (which protects an individual from incriminating himself) provided ammunition for critics who charged that he was willing to trample upon the safeguards provided in the Constitution in the pursuit of what he believed was right.

Kennedy resigned from the Rackets Committee in September 1959 in order to take charge of his brother's campaign for the presidency. John Kennedy had been mentioned as the front-runner for the Democratic nomination since shortly after Stevenson's defeat in 1956. Hubert Humphrey, the liberal senator from Minnesota, intended to challenge Kennedy in the primaries, and Senate Majority Leader Lyndon Johnson was expected to make a bid for the nomination at the convention.

Putting to use the lessons he had learned watching Stevenson mishandle his campaign, Kennedy worked his staff relentlessly, operating on the principle that a campaign had only so many days and that a day lost at the start could not be made up later. Despite the image of the "Kennedy machine," Robert Kennedy's genius as campaign manager lay not so much in long-range planning as in assessing situations as they arose and improvising the next step. However, one element that contributed to the machine image — Joseph Kennedy's willingness to fund his son's campaign — proved helpful. While Humphrey and his entourage traveled from town to town in a beat-up bus, Kennedy and his entourage flew in a private plane — named the *Caroline*, after John's daughter — donated by Joseph Kennedy. In

[He was] absolutely strong, steel-willed, didn't mind telling a mayor of a city or governor or anyone else what he thought if he stepped out of line. He just was blunt and hard and tough and was of course a magnificent campaign manager.
—JOSEPH TYDINGS
senator of Maryland, on Robert Kennedy during the 1960 presidential campaign

West Virginia, where contributions to local politicians by presidential candidates were a cherished tradition, Joseph Kennedy's were extremely generous.

Despite his many assets, John Kennedy had several liabilities as a candidate. The most serious were his relative youth — he was 42 in the campaign's early days — and the widespread perception that a Catholic could not be elected president. It was thus essential that he make a strong showing in the primaries to demonstrate to the governors, mayors, and party leaders who would control delegates at the convention that he had sufficient popular support to overcome these drawbacks and win the November election.

Kennedy took Wisconsin, the site of the first primary, but not overwhelmingly. West Virginia, where it was said a Catholic could not be elected dogcatcher, loomed as a major challenge. Kennedy met it head-on, telling voters, "Nobody asked me if I was a Catholic when I joined the United States Navy." John's honesty in confronting the religion issue, Robert's hard work, their father's deep pockets, the endorsement of Franklin Roosevelt, Jr. (West Virginians fondly remembered the New Deal), and support among black voters (Senator Robert Byrd, a former member of the Ku Klux Klan, endorsed Humphrey) combined to give Kennedy a smashing victory that drove Humphrey from the race. West Virginia was also important because it provided the brothers with their first glimpse of the type of entrenched poverty that remained unseen by so many Americans. Friends remember Robert Kennedy expressing disbelief and amazement that conditions such as those he discovered in the hills and hollows of Appalachia existed in America in the 20th century. "Can you believe it?" he asked over and over again. "Some of those kids have never had a glass of milk."

At the convention in Los Angeles, John Kennedy won the nomination on the first ballot. Robert was characteristically indefatigable, staying up for three consecutive nights to ensure that all the delegates were counted and in place. The only problem involved the selection of a vice-president. Robert Kennedy vehemently opposed Johnson as a running mate. John was similarly unenthusiastic, recognizing Johnson's unacceptability to labor and civil rights groups. Because Johnson was popular in the southern states, whose support was essential for a Democratic victory in November, John Kennedy felt that he should be offered the position, particularly as it was believed that the powerful Senate leader had no interest in the vice-presidency. The hope was that such a gesture would ensure the Kennedy candidacy of Johnson's enthusiastic support. To the chagrin of the Kennedy brothers, Johnson accepted. Robert was assigned the undesirable task of persuading Johnson to reconsider. His unsuccessful effort was the first episode in a series of differences and misunderstandings between the two men that would develop into mutual rancor.

The Republican candidates were Richard Nixon, Eisenhower's vice-president, who had first come to prominence as a California congressman employing the same type of red-baiting tactics as McCarthy, and Kennedy's old Massachusetts political opponent Henry Cabot Lodge, Jr. Age and religion were again issues. Although Nixon was just four years older, he contrasted his vast foreign policy experience as vice-president with Kennedy's youth, but when the two met for nationally televised debates, it was the younger man who appeared more poised, self-assured, and in command of himself and the issues. Kennedy laid the issue of his religion to rest with a speech to the Greater Houston Ministerial Association. Seeking to dismiss unfounded beliefs that a Catholic president would be subservient to the pope and other religious leaders, Kennedy emphatically stated his belief in the separation of church and state and pledged to make decisions "without regard to outside religious pressures or dictates."

Perhaps the most important issue of the campaign was civil rights. Inspired by the Reverend Martin Luther King, Jr., and other religious leaders, blacks in the South had become increasingly active in demanding equal rights — to education, housing,

Robert Kennedy suggested that his brother put to rest the issue of his religion with a campaign appearance before the Greater Houston Ministerial Association, where John Kennedy assured the 500 assembled members of the group that as president his first duty would be to the country and the Constitution, not the pope.

John Kennedy and his wife, the former Jacqueline Bouvier, on the way to his inauguration in January 1961. A youthful elan, optimism, and practical idealism were to be the hallmarks of the Kennedy administration.

employment, the vote, to freedom from arbitrary arrest and lynching. They demanded an end to discrimination and segregation. Although prejudice and troubled race relations were not confined to the South, that region — where segregation was codified both legally and socially — was the focus of the civil rights movement in its early days.

The Kennedy interest in civil rights at that time was political; there was no great commitment to the principle. The importance of the black vote had been demonstrated to the Kennedys in West Virginia, but they were also acutely conscious of the danger of alienating white southern voters. However, John Kennedy also had to court the votes of white northern liberals, many of whom were concerned about civil rights. As a result he insisted on including a strong civil rights plank in the Democratic party platform, which Robert told campaign workers the candidate "unequivocally" supported and described as the best the party had ever had.

One month before the election Martin Luther King, Jr., was arrested at an Atlanta department store where he and other blacks were staging a sit-in to protest the store's segregated lunch counters. On parole for a minor traffic infraction, King was sentenced to four months in a labor camp for parole violation. He was taken to prison in leg irons and handcuffs. King's supporters were concerned for his safety. Lynching, beating, or an "accidental" death were real possibilities. When John Kennedy learned of King's wife's concern, he called to console her. Worried that his brother's action would cost him three southern states in the impending election, Robert Kennedy was initially critical, but when he learned that King had been denied the opportunity to post bail, his sense of justice was offended. He telephoned the judge involved and registered his feelings. King was released the next day.

As the campaign wound down, Robert Kennedy pushed himself and his staffers even harder. Irritated Democratic party workers warned each other that "Little Brother is watching you." He was the man who said no to party bosses, who chewed out mayors and governors when they fell short of his standards. A famous exchange that took place in New York illustrates his determination and sense of priorities. Annoyed at the squabbling over local issues that was interfering with the smooth operation of his brother's campaign, Kennedy told a roomful of party regulars, "I don't give a damn if the state and county organizations survive after November. I don't give a damn if *you* survive. I want to elect John F. Kennedy." In November John Kennedy was elected president by an extremely narrow margin. He won the popular vote by less than one-tenth of one percent, and in several states black votes made the difference.

The more I thought about the injustice of it, the more I thought what a son of a bitch that judge was. I made it clear to him that it was not a political call; that I am a lawyer, one who believes in the rights of all defendants to make bond and one who had seen the rights of defendants misused in various ways . . . and I wanted to make it clear that I opposed this. I felt it was disgraceful.
—ROBERT KENNEDY on his phone call protesting Martin Luther King, Jr.'s, imprisonment in 1960

4

The Attorney General

The president-elect wanted his younger brother to join his cabinet as attorney general, but Robert Kennedy declined, saying that he had been "chasing bad guys for three years" with the Rackets Committee. When John persisted, citing the sacrifices others were making to join the administration and his own need for someone on whom he could rely, someone he knew well, who would speak the hard truth when difficult situations demanded it, Robert accepted. The appointment was controversial. As attorney general, Robert Kennedy was the nation's chief law enforcement officer, responsible for overseeing the Department of Justice, the Bureau of Prisons, the Department of Alcohol, Tobacco and Firearms, the Border Patrol, and the FBI. Many believed he was unsuited for the position, charging that he was young, inexperienced, and had never practiced law. The president joked that he would make the announcement by opening the front door of his Washington townhouse at 2:00 A.M. one morning, look up and down the street to make certain no one was there, and then whisper, "It's Bobby."

I don't see what's wrong with giving Bobby a little experience before he goes into law practice.
—JOHN KENNEDY
after naming his brother attorney general

Although initially reluctant to accept an appointment as attorney general in his brother's cabinet, Robert Kennedy would prove to be the second most important member of the Kennedy administration.

Segregation was enforced by law in most southern states in the early 1960s. Believing a Congress in which white southerners held important positions would not pass effective civil rights legislation, the Kennedys initially favored using the courts to secure voting rights long denied to southern blacks.

Kennedy introduced his own personal touch to an agency historically known for its starched-shirt stodginess. He was often found with his coat off, shirt sleeves rolled up, and his feet up on his mahogany desk. The walls of his spacious office were decorated with watercolors by his children. He walked the halls, stopped in offices, spoke to everyone, and extended his reach outside Washington to staffers throughout the country. Most important, under his direction the Justice Department was instilled with a passion for hard work and quality results, and his talented staff spent long hours maintaining very high professional standards.

The most serious domestic issue facing the country was civil rights, and it is on his record in this area that Kennedy's leadership of the Justice Department must be judged. There is little doubt that in his early days in the administration Kennedy saw civil rights as an abstract political issue and possessed little understanding of its greater importance. Kennedy said later that at that time he "didn't lose much sleep about Negroes, I didn't think about them much, I didn't know about all the injustice."

Although he regarded segregation as wrong, he believed integration could proceed only as rapidly as the time it took to change the attitudes of white southerners and implement change through the judicial and political systems. He did not understand that for blacks — systematically denied the right to live where they wanted, to fair and full employment, to freedom of movement and association, to vote, and to the same opportunities for a full and meaningful life as enjoyed by white Americans — the issue carried much greater urgency.

Recognizing that comprehensive civil rights legislation would not win approval by a Congress in which several key committee chairmanships were held by southerners, President Kennedy made executive action the keystone of his early civil rights policy. Believing that participation in elections would enable blacks to attain other goals, voting rights became the focus of the administration's efforts. Throughout the South intimidation and fraudulent tactics such as improperly administered poll taxes and literacy tests were used to deny blacks the vote. The administration's approach was to sue individual states, as well as county and local jurisdictions, to force them to allow blacks to exercise their right to the ballot. Kennedy dispatched Justice Department attorneys throughout the South to gather testimony and prepare and argue the 57 voting-rights suits the department brought. (That number was more than nine times as many as brought by the Eisenhower administration.)

The problem with such an approach was the length of time it took for such suits to progress through the court system. Southern state governments used the appeals process and obfuscatory tactics to delay final verdicts and often simply ignored them once they were handed down. What progress the Justice Department did achieve was negated somewhat by Kennedy's appointment of racist judges in the South. Because Kennedy's appointees to the federal bench had to be approved by the Senate Judiciary Committee, chaired by James Eastland of Mississippi, he often found it necessary to approve racists recommended by Eastland and

Senator James Eastland of Mississippi was the influential chairman of the Senate Judiciary Committee. Kennedy often had to accept Eastland's choices for federal judgeships — many of whom were racists — in order to obtain the Judiciary Committee's approval of his own more progressive nominees for other federal judiciary spots.

The sit-in, as practiced by these blacks at a whites-only lunch counter in Little Rock, Arkansas, in November 1962, was one tactic used by civil rights activists to draw attention to the ongoing injustice of racial discrimination. Critics of Kennedy's Justice Department charged that it provided insufficient protection for those involved in the civil rights movement, many of whom were the targets of violence.

other southern senators in order to gain approval of his own black and liberal appointees. The realities of practical politics were little consolation to the black applicants in a voting-rights suit who heard one of Kennedy's judges denounce them as "a bunch of niggers . . . acting like a bunch of chimpanzees." Blacks questioned whether Kennedy's trade-off was worth it when another of his appointees called the Supreme Court decision ending segregation in public schools "one of the truly regrettable decisions of all time."

The civil rights movement gathered a momentum that outstripped the deliberate speed with which the federal government wished to move. Black determination to achieve the full measure of what had been promised them in the Constitution but long denied them in practice collided head-on with white America's reluctance to change. An early attempt by the freedom riders — black and white civil rights activists — to use a bus trip through seven southern states to desegregate lunch counters and washrooms in bus terminals was met with violence. Their bus was burned in Anniston, Alabama, and they were beaten with baseball bats, pipes, and chains in Birmingham. In Montgomery the group was again attacked, and one of Kennedy's assistants who had been sent to report on the situation was knocked unconscious. Kennedy finally was forced to dispatch the National Guard to Montgomery to restore order. The immediate crisis over, Kennedy used his relationship with Eastland and other southern politicians to arrange guarantees of safety for the rest of the freedom riders' trip. Several months later he persuaded the Interstate Commerce Commission to issue a regulation banning segregation in bus terminals.

The violence that befell the freedom riders was a not uncommon fate of civil rights activists in the South during the early 1960s. Blacks and whites working to register voters or otherwise active in the movement were subject to arbitrary arrest and imprisonment, harassment, intimidation, beatings, and even murder. Kennedy's Justice Department was often charged with failing to provide such individuals with sufficient protection. The argument that the Constitution reserved police power for local authorities and that federal law then provided little basis for intervention by the national government was of little comfort to those whose lives were being threatened. Even Robert Kennedy himself admitted that "careful explanations of the historic limitations on the federal government's police powers are not satisfactory to the parents of students who have vanished in Mississippi or to the widow of a Negro educator shot down without any reason by night riders in Georgia."

Governor Ross Barnett of Mississippi believed that attempts by the federal government to protect blacks' civil rights were an unlawful interference with the rights of the individual southern states. Barnett allowed James Meredith, a black man, to enroll at the University of Mississippi only after President Kennedy sent federal troops to the campus.

Beneath a drawing by his young son David, a harried Kennedy confers with his aide Nicholas Katzenbach in May 1961. The topic was the situation in Montgomery, Alabama, where the National Guard had been sent to restore order following a series of attacks and threats against civil rights workers.

Kennedy said soon after taking office that as he believed all people were created equal, it followed that integration should occur immediately everywhere, but that one had to take into consideration that "other people have grown up with totally different attitudes and mores, which we can't change overnight." After almost two years at the Justice Department, Kennedy began to understand the intransigence of such different attitudes and mores. Armed with a court order and Supreme Court affirmation, in September 1962 James Meredith attempted to become the first black man to enroll at the University of Mississippi. Avowing the doctrine of states' rights and publicly proclaiming defiance, Governor Ross Barnett personally blocked Meredith's path several times when he attempted to register. Kennedy's negotiations with Barnett proved fruitless. On the afternoon of Sunday, September 30, Justice Department attorneys Nicholas Katzenbach and John Doar and a group of federal marshals found themselves surrounded by an angry mob outside the University of Mississippi administrative office. As night fell the crowd grew in size and began throwing bricks and bottles. Gunshots were heard, and Katzenbach authorized the marshals to fire tear gas. As the evening wore on, the tear gas ran out and the mob grew increasingly unruly. Two people were killed, 137 marshals were injured, and 29 marshals and 13 members of the Mississippi National Guard, which the president had federalized, were shot. Katzenbach asked that the army be sent to restore order. The marshals hung on through the night, until the army's arrival quieted things. Meredith registered that morning at 8:00 A.M.

The vehemence of the hatred expressed by Mississippi's racists stunned Kennedy. When in the early summer of 1963 Alabama governor George Wallace — vowing "Segregation now! Segregation tomorrow! Segregation forever!" — promised to block the registration of black students at the state university, Robert Kennedy convinced Alabama business leaders to express to the governor their disapproval of his show of defiance. Kennedy himself told Wallace of his intention to uphold the law and hinted at the use of troops. When the black students appeared on campus on June 11, 1963, escorted by Nicholas Katzenbach, Wallace backed down.

Kennedy's experience of the virulence of racism as practiced in the South helped him to understand somewhat the despair felt by black Americans, as did his meeting with several of America's most prominent black writers and artists in May 1963. Among those attending were novelist and essayist James Baldwin, singers Lena Horne and Harry Belafonte, sociologist Kenneth Clark, and playwright Lorraine Hansberry, as well as a young civil rights worker, Jerome Smith, who had spent many months in jail for his activities. Kennedy had expected a reasoned discussion of possible programs and legislation, but the afternoon turned into an impassioned discussion of the pain of being black in America and the hatred and rage many blacks felt for white America, including the Kennedy administration. Kennedy's attempts to steer the conversation to concrete proposals were scoffed at as the meeting became, in the words of Clark, "one of the most violent, emotional verbal assaults . . . that I had ever witnessed before or since." Kennedy was embittered and frustrated by the encounter, but it certainly brought home to him that for black Americans the civil rights question possessed an urgency that far transcended that attached to an abstract political issue.

One of the most powerful men in government, FBI director J. Edgar Hoover was obsessed with the danger of domestic subversion. Asserting that the civil rights movement was under communist influence, Hoover convinced Robert Kennedy to approve wiretaps on Martin Luther King, Jr., and other civil rights leaders.

In August 1963 hundreds of thousands of Americans, white and black, came to Washington, D.C., to demonstrate in support of civil rights. The March on Washington's climax came with Martin Luther King's (front, center) famous "I Have a Dream" speech.

On the night of June 11, 1963 — the same day Wallace stepped aside at the University of Alabama — John Kennedy made a televised address to the nation in which he announced that he was sending a comprehensive civil rights bill to Congress. With a good portion of the nation outraged by recent events in Birmingham, Alabama — where Sheriff Eugene "Bull" Connor had turned fire hoses and unleashed attack dogs on marchers led by Martin Luther King — the president hoped that public opinion had been swayed enough to enable his legislation to pass. Of all the president's cabinet officers and close advisers, only Robert Kennedy supported sending the legislation to Congress at that time. His comments after the bombing of a Birmingham church killed four young black girls indicated how much his attitudes had changed. He said that though two Klansmen might have been responsible for the bombing, "in the last analysis . . . it's Governor Barnett and Jim Eastland and John Stennis and the business community. . . . It's George Wallace and political and business leaders and newspapers. . . . They're the ones that created the climate that made those kinds of actions possible. . . . With all the smiles and all the graciousness of Dick Russell and Herman Talmadge and Jim Eastland and George Smathers and [Spessard] Holland . . . none of them really made any effort to counter this." [The names mentioned were all southern senators and governors.]

Kennedy's most dramatic failure as attorney general concerned his stewardship of the FBI and his relationship with J. Edgar Hoover, the bureau's longtime director. Hoover became head of the FBI in 1924, the year before Kennedy was born, and his many years in Washington and storehouse of information on people made him one of the capital's most feared individuals. A stodgy, ruthless, conservative man, his racist assumptions and obsession with communism corrupted a good deal of the bureau's work. Although nominally subordinate to the attorney general, Hoover functioned more or less autonomously. Kennedy wanted the FBI to concentrate its efforts on organized crime, but Hoover was more concerned with padding the bureau's arrest statistics and with what he believed was communist subversion of the civil rights movement.

Hoover was obsessed with King. In 1962 the FBI designated King a communist who was to be interned in case of a national emergency. After the March on Washington in August 1963 and King's "I have a dream" speech, Hoover denounced the civil rights leader as "the most dangerous Negro of the future in this nation." Shortly after King became the youngest American to win the Nobel Peace Prize, in 1964, Hoover characterized him as the "most notorious liar" in the country. Although Kennedy knew that Hoover's charges of communist infiltration of King's organization were groundless, he approved the director's request for wiretaps on the phones of King and his associates. Kennedy believed that allowing Hoover to listen to King's conversations was the best way to demonstrate to him the baselessness of his charges, clear King of suspicion, and prevent Hoover from releasing rumors and innuendo that would destroy any chance the civil rights bill had of passing. Although Hoover did not discover evidence of subversion, he was able to compile evidence that King was engaging in adulterous activity and used that material in an outright attempt to blackmail King into ceasing his civil rights efforts. Kennedy's role in the wiretappings provided his critics with yet another example of his purported insensitivity to civil liberties issues — as did his renewed investigation of Jimmy Hoffa — and his alleged willingness to employ dubious means to achieve his desired ends.

> *J. Edgar Hoover had the racist instincts of a white man who had grown up in Washington when it was still a southern city.*
> —ARTHUR M. SCHLESINGER, JR.
> Kennedy biographer

5

The President's Man

Besides serving as attorney general, Robert Kennedy was the president's man, his most trusted and closest adviser. Because there were few major decisions on which the attorney general's counsel was not sought, his influence was felt throughout the government. He enjoyed virtually unlimited access to the president, visited the Oval Office often, and conferred on the telephone with his brother up to 5 or 10 times a day. The president relied on Robert for a number of reasons. He knew that Robert would tell him his honest opinion and not just what he thought the president wanted to hear. He saw Robert as an extraordinarily compassionate man whose thoughts and actions were guided by principles of fairness and the strictest personal ethics. At the same time the president respected his brother's toughness, the stamina that allowed him to work long hours without tiring, his ability to keep his cool in times of crisis, and his capacity for dispassionate analysis of emotion-laden issues and situations. Recognizing his own impatience in dealing with administrative details, the president depended on Robert's organizational skills. In a government filled with men who had ideas, John Kennedy saw

The president has to take so much responsibility that others should move forward to take the blame. People want someone higher to appeal to. . . . It is better for ire and anger to be directed somewhere else.
—ROBERT KENNEDY
on his role in his brother's administration

President Kennedy inspects missile sites at Key West, Florida, in 1962. In the autumn of that year the Soviet Union installed nuclear missiles in Cuba, just 90 miles away, triggering a tense confrontation between the world's two most powerful nations.

Robert as that rarest of commodities — a man who accomplished things. Foreign policy adviser Chester Bowles remarked that the president's idea of good management was to call his brother and say, "Here are ten things I want to get done." Nowhere was Robert Kennedy's role as the president's man more evident than in the administration's relations with the island nation of Cuba, which involved him in two of the most serious crises of the Kennedy presidency.

Although the age of McCarthyism had passed, cold war rhetoric and thought still informed the nation's foreign policy, and the ongoing economic and political competition with the Soviet Union was seen as the most important foreign policy issue. While

Cuban militiamen undergo inspection. Alarmed by Cuban leader Fidel Castro's drift toward communism and friendship with the leaders of the Soviet Union, the Kennedys approved a CIA-sponsored invasion of Cuba in April 1961, but the well-prepared Cuban military routed the strike force, taking most of its members prisoner.

advocating a realistic appraisal of the United States's ability to counter communist-backed military aggression and the use of economic and social programs to win the hearts and minds of third world nations and sway them toward capitalism, the Kennedys accepted many of the cold war era's basic assumptions. John's inaugural address announced his determination to meet any challenges offered by the communist nations while extending the possibility of a more flexible and conciliatory approach: "Let every nation know . . . that we shall pay any price, bear any burden, meet any hardship, support any friend, oppose any foe, to assure the survival and success of liberty. . . . Let us never negotiate out of fear, but let us never fear to negotiate."

That determination was first tested by events in Cuba, where Fidel Castro had taken power from U.S.-supported dictator Fulgencio Batista shortly after the new year in 1959. Castro made friendly overtures toward the United States, but when the Eisenhower administration proved suspicious of the new leader, he turned to the Soviet Union for funds to develop Cuba's agricultural economy. Alarmed by his appropriation of American property in Cuba, his intention of reforming the Cuban economy, his apparent friendliness with the Soviet Union, and the possibility of a communist regime just 90 miles from Florida, the Eisenhower administration resolved to oust Castro. The Central Intelligence Agency (CIA) and Joint Chiefs of Staff of the military drew up a plan that would utilize anti-Castro Cuban exiles for an invasion of their former homeland.

The decision of Soviet premier Nikita Khrushchev (third from right) to remove his country's missiles from Cuba without consulting Castro (center, with beard) greatly damaged the relationship between the two leaders, although they did enjoy this lighthearted moment together during Castro's visit to the Soviet Union in January 1964.

Kennedy took office before Eisenhower could put the plan into effect, but the proposed operation had now gathered its own momentum. Exiled Cubans were being trained and armed by the CIA for the proposed invasion. Both Kennedys were briefed on the details. A small force of approximately 1,500 men was to land at the Bay of Pigs, on Cuba's southern coast. They would then fight their way onto the beach — although little resistance was expected — and disappear into the nearby hills, where as guerrillas they would lead the popular uprising against Castro that the operation's planners believed would accompany news of the invasion. Assured by the Joint Chiefs and the CIA that the plan had a two-thirds chance of success and fearful that failure to give the go-ahead would result in Republican criticism that the new president was soft on communism, both brothers approved the operation.

Throughout the entire period of the crisis, a period of the most intense strain I have ever operated under, he [Kennedy] remained calm and cool, firm but restrained, never nettled and never rattled.

—ROBERT MCNAMARA secretary of defense during the Kennedy administration, on Robert Kennedy's composure during the Cuban missile crisis

I don't think it's going as well as it should.
—JOHN KENNEDY
to Robert Kennedy on the
Bay of Pigs invasion

Little went as planned. The attack occurred shortly after midnight on April 17, 1961. Despite the plan's supposed secrecy, Castro was expecting an incursion and had deployed his forces accordingly. Reconnaissance of the landing site was faulty, and the invaders found themselves hopelessly bogged down in the swamps that ringed the beaches. Castro's air force sunk several of the force's ammunition ships, and soon the entire landing brigade was surrounded. Recognizing that the invasion was an unsalvageable disaster, the president canceled a proposed supporting air strike. Nearly 1,200 men were taken prisoner.

Recrimination and accusation followed. Depending on the speaker, the president was either a reckless adventurer or had suffered a failure of nerve. Robert Kennedy was assigned to preside over the aftermath. Although retired general Maxwell Taylor was the official chairman of the Cuba Study Group, for the next six weeks Robert Kennedy took the lead in investigating witnesses and otherwise determining reasons for the disaster. Not surprisingly, he concluded that the majority of the blame belonged to the Joint Chiefs of Staff for their insufficient reconnaissance, shoddy planning, and failure to "properly examine all of the military ramifications" of the operation or devote "adequate study and attention" to its execution.

Castro's presence continued to gall the Kennedys. Emphasizing that "a solution to the Cuban problem today carries top priority in the United States government; no time, money, effort or manpower is to be spared," Robert Kennedy expressed his approval of a new program, Operation Mongoose, which used CIA-trained Cuban exiles as operatives in a program of sabotage directed against refineries, factories, shipping, and other economic targets within Cuba. Used to operating in a semiautonomous fashion, the CIA also apparently interpreted the Kennedy brothers' pronouncements on Cuba as an approval for assassination attempts they made on Castro.

The Cuban crisis came to a head in October 1962. On the 15th of that month reconnaissance photos revealed the presence of nuclear missile sites in

Cuba. Premier Nikita Khrushchev of the Soviet Union had provided Castro with nuclear bombers, surface-to-surface medium- and intermediate-range nuclear missiles, and 22,000 Soviet troops. The nuclear missiles were by far the most worrisome problem for the United States. Khrushchev was gambling that Kennedy would not respond to his provocation, but the president had no intention of allowing the Soviet Union to extend its influence by establishing a nuclear presence in the Western Hemisphere.

In the tense days that followed, the Executive Committee of the National Security Council, composed of the president's top aides and advisers, pondered the U.S. response. The Joint Chiefs of Staff and several others, including Maxwell Taylor, Dean Acheson, John McCloy, Paul Nitze, Douglas Dillon, and John McCone, advocated an immediate bombing raid to eliminate the missiles. Robert Kennedy vehemently opposed the proposal. He was not about, he said, to let his brother go down in the history books as that era's Tojo (the architect of the Japanese attack on Pearl Harbor that brought the United States into World War II). Instead, Kennedy advocated a naval blockade, or quarantine, that would attempt to deny access to Cuba to the Soviet ships bearing the warheads that would make the missiles operational. The debate raged back and forth for five days, with Kennedy unable to "accept the idea that the United States would rain bombs on Cuba, killing thousands and thousands of civilians in a surprise attack." On the 20th the president opted for a quarantine. Four days later two Soviet ships approached the U.S. blockade, stopped, and turned back.

The problem now became the removal of the missiles already in place. The president cabled Khrushchev on the 25th with his wish that the Soviet leader would allow a "restoration of the earlier situation." Tension lifted on the 26th with the receipt of Khrushchev's response expressing his concern about the danger of the present confrontation between the superpowers and hinting that the Soviet missiles might be removed in exchange for a U.S.

I said I did not believe the president of the United States could order such a military operation. I said we were fighting for something more than just military survival and that all our heritage and our ideals would be repugnant to such a sneak military attack.
—ROBERT KENNEDY
on his position during the Cuban missile crisis

In January 1963, Kennedy was honored by veterans of the Bay of Pigs invasion for his efforts in securing the release of participants in that operation taken captive by Castro. Kennedy led the effort to raise the $53 million in medical supplies and foodstuffs that Castro demanded as ransom.

guarantee that it would not invade Cuba. On the 27th a second, more belligerent missive from Khrushchev arrived, demanding the removal of U.S. missiles in Turkey. This second letter created a quandary among the president's advisers, with the hardliners insisting upon the impossibility of relinquishing the Turkish missiles. Robert Kennedy broke the stalemate by proposing that the president respond positively to Khrushchev's first, conciliatory offer. He then drafted the text of the president's message. Some hours after the president's letter was sent, an exhausted Kennedy — he had not slept in days — met with Soviet ambassador Anatoly Dobrynin at the Department of Justice. Kennedy reiterated the U.S. position. When Dobrynin mentioned the Turkish missiles, Kennedy replied that he could not make their removal part of any deal, but he assured Dobrynin that the missiles would come out some months in the future, adding that the United States would not feel obligated to abide by this portion of the agreement were the Soviet Union to make it public. (The president had decided some months earlier that the Turkish missiles were obsolete and had been pushing for their withdrawal.) The next day Khrushchev announced that he was withdrawing the nuclear weapons, bringing the Cuban missile crisis to an end.

Kennedy's work on Cuba did not end with the resolution of the missile crisis. He now returned his attention to arranging for the release of the 1,150 prisoners taken captive during the Bay of Pigs invasion. Earlier negotiations with Castro had proved difficult, with the Cuban leader demanding 500 heavy-construction bulldozers in exchange for the prisoners' release. Objecting that the type of bulldozers requested seemed especially well-suited for military construction, a committee formed by Kennedy proposed agricultural equipment instead. Castro said he would prefer the dollar value of the bulldozers — $28 million. With Republican congressmen criticizing the payment of any sort of "indemnity" by the United States, the deal fell through. In April 1962 Castro did agree to release 60 sick and injured prisoners in exchange for $2.9 million, which Kennedy raised independently.

Having received reports that many of the prisoners were in extremely poor physical and psychological condition, Kennedy renewed his efforts on their behalf with a new vigor after the missile crisis. With Castro now demanding drugs and medical goods, Kennedy turned his energy to convincing medical supply firms to donate the items Castro had specified, a task complicated by an ongoing congressional investigation of the drug industry that had left pharmaceutical executives mistrustful of the Kennedy administration. The supplies obtained, Kennedy then had to arrange the complicated logistics of the transfer. Released prisoners began arriving in Florida about one week before Christmas 1962; the last were given their freedom on Christmas Eve.

The 10 or 12 people who had participated in these discussions were bright and energetic people. We had perhaps amongst the most able in the country and if any one of half a dozen of them were president the world would have been very likely plunged into a catastrophic war.
—ROBERT KENNEDY
on the deliberations during
the Cuban missile crisis

79

6

"We Are All Participants"

John Kennedy was shot and killed in Dallas, Texas, on November 22, 1963. His death stunned the nation and left his brother "the most shattered man I had ever seen in my life," according to his close friend and presidential press secretary Pierre Salinger. Robert Kennedy had spent much of his adult life looking out for his older brother's interests, and John's death left him adrift. He lost himself in long walks, lengthy reveries, and reading, finding particular consolation in poetry and the works of the Greek tragedians Sophocles, Euripides, and Aeschylus, as well as the French novelist Albert Camus. A colleague from the Justice Department, John Seigenthaler, described the palpable sense of physical pain that Kennedy's grief exuded: "I just had the feeling that it was physically painful, almost as if he were on the rack or that he had a toothache or that he had a heart attack. I mean it was pain and it showed itself as being pain. . . . It was very obvious to me, almost when he got up to walk that it hurt to get up to walk."

> The assassination [of John Kennedy] punctured the center of Robert Kennedy's universe.
> —JACK NEWFIELD
> Kennedy biographer and friend

A pensive Robert Kennedy outside a Northampton, Massachusetts, hospital where his brother Edward had been brought on June 19, 1964, after being severely injured in a plane crash. With his brother John dead and his father disabled by a stroke, Robert had increased responsibility in Kennedy family matters.

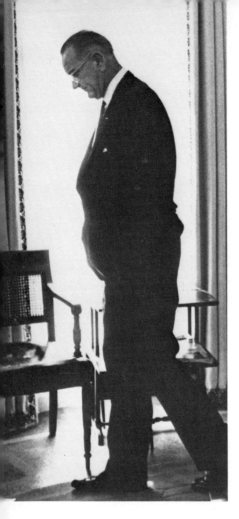

Lyndon Johnson succeeded John Kennedy as president. Although Johnson and Robert Kennedy disliked each other intensely, Kennedy was initially a strong supporter of Johnson's progressive domestic programs, which were known collectively as the Great Society.

The political life of the country continued. Lyndon Johnson became president immediately upon Kennedy's death. The day after the shooting Johnson asked Robert Kennedy to stay on as attorney general, telling him, "I need you more than the president needed you." Kennedy acquiesced, but his heart was not in it. The prosecutorial zeal that so enraged his enemies had gone with his brother's death. He was unable even to take satisfaction in two criminal convictions of Jimmy Hoffa.

Kennedy's feelings about Johnson only exacerbated his sense of loss. He had never cared for the Texan, considering him too much the consummate politician, the wheeler-dealer ever ready to compromise, and was disenchanted by Johnson's monumental ego and insecurities, his craving for attention, and what Kennedy believed was his utter inability to tell the truth. Appalled by Johnson's lack of constructive advice at times of crisis — during the confrontation over the Cuban missiles, for example — and on crucial issues such as civil rights, Kennedy felt the vice-president had contributed little to the administration's success. Underlying all was his grief and sense of resentment at seeing Johnson occupy the office that Kennedy believed rightfully was his brother's. Certain actions by Johnson in the immediate aftermath of the shooting in Dallas — insisting on being sworn in within an hour after John Kennedy's death and ordering the former president's secretary to remove her things by 9:30 on the morning following the slaying — fueled such feelings in the emotional Kennedy.

Johnson harbored a similarly strong dislike for Kennedy. He was unable to forget that it was Robert Kennedy who had tried to convince him to withdraw his acceptance of the vice-presidential nomination. An astute politician and extremely capable former leader of the Senate, Johnson chafed under the limitations inherent in his role as vice-president — in which he had no real responsibility — and bridled at Kennedy's closeness to the president, the widespread perception that Kennedy was the number-two man in the government, and the belief, as expressed by presidential aide Richard Goodwin, that it was Robert Kennedy who had "made the greatest contribution to the success and historical reputation of [John Kennedy's] administration." Expansive and garrulous, Johnson worried that he appeared unpolished and unsophisticated compared to the smooth, self-contained Ivy Leaguers who filled the Kennedy White House. The transition period was particularly difficult for the insecure Johnson. John Kennedy's aides, his brother included, were notable for their fierce loyalty to him. With the shock of his death, they regarded themselves as the protectors of his programs and legacy. Johnson perceived this keeping of the flame as implying that in some way his presidency was not quite legitimate and believed that Robert Kennedy was the chief author of such sentiment: "Then Kennedy was killed and I became the custodian of his will. I became the president. But none of this seemed to register with Bobby Kennedy, who acted like he was the custodian of the Kennedy dream, some sort of rightful heir to the Kennedy throne."

Rejected by Johnson as a vice-presidential candidate in 1964, Kennedy decided to run for the Senate from New York, although he did not reside in the state. He is shown here marching in New York City's Columbus Day Parade — a traditional appearance by campaigning politicians — with his sons Robert, Jr., (left) and David.

Kennedy in the Mississippi Delta. Although Kennedy was often villified by conservatives as a liberal, his concern for the poor arose less from fixed political ideology than from a personal response to human suffering and basic need.

The mutual unease continued into the spring of 1964, Kennedy resentful at Johnson's taking credit for programs his brother had initiated, Johnson doubtful of Kennedy's loyalty. Nevertheless, as the primaries approached, Kennedy was often mentioned as the most likely running mate for Johnson in the fall election. Polls showed him to be the preference of a majority of Democrats. Hopeful that the election would provide him with a mandate that would remove him from the slain president's shadow, Johnson did not wish to have Kennedy on his ticket, although he conceded he would take Kennedy if that was the price of victory. Kennedy was unable to make up his mind as to whether he wanted the nomination. Although he saw the merit of remaining as a spokesman for his brother's ideas within the Johnson administration, he also felt that as vice-president he would be powerless to affect policy. With polls showing a probable victory in November even without Kennedy, Johnson summoned him to the White House in late July and broke the news that he would not be on the ticket. Anticipating the decision, Kennedy had already determined to resign from the cabinet and seek the Senate seat of New York's Kenneth Keating.

The decision brought new charges of ruthlessness, for Kennedy did not live in New York State but in McLean, Virginia, at Hickory Hill, the home he had purchased from his brother John. Newspapers, particularly the *New York Times*, accused him of carpetbagging, of using New York as a stepping-stone toward a future run for the presidency. Wary of Kennedy, many liberal Democrats deserted the party in favor of Keating, who had a good voting record on civil rights, but they soon discovered that the Kennedy name was magic. Despite being in some ways an indifferent campaigner — he was a notoriously poor reader of prepared texts, and his shyness often caused him to mumble and stammer and his hands to shake — Kennedy drew large and enthusiastic crowds seemingly unconcerned by the carpetbagging charges. At a state convention of the National Association for the Advancement of Colored People (NAACP), after Keating accused Kennedy of "abandoning" the civil rights movement by resigning from the Justice Department, Charles Evers, head of the Mississippi branch of the NAACP, told the audience they were "fortunate to have a man of Kennedy's caliber even visit New York, much less running for senator. Bobby Kennedy means more for us in Mississippi than any white man I know." Kennedy was elected to the Senate by a large margin in November.

Fierce rioting in predominantly black urban areas occurred each summer from 1965 to 1968. These National Guardsmen were sent to Detroit to quell the disorder there in July 1967. Alarmed by the violence, many politicians called for a renewed commitment to "law and order."

Kennedy in his Senate office, before giving his March 1967 speech in which he called for an end to the U.S. bombing of North Vietnam. Although Kennedy was not the first senator to state his objections to the Vietnam War, he soon became one of the most influential political leaders in opposition to U.S. involvement in the conflict.

He was perhaps the best-known first-term senator ever to serve in that institution. His Senate offices had an undergraduate atmosphere to them — cramped, cluttered, alive with enthusiasm and activity. The office received more than 1,000 pieces of mail a day and was so busy that Kennedy personally paid $100,000 a year beyond the official allowance in order to hire extra help. The young and energetic staff worked six and sometimes seven days a week.

Robert Kennedy had never had a political agenda of his own. The ideas and issues with which he had been associated were largely the result of circumstance and his close association with his brother. Although often reviled, particularly by white southerners, for his supposed liberalism, in truth he had little fixed ideology. If as a child of the New Deal era he had an inherent belief in the capacity of government to effect positive change for its citizens, he had also inherited his father's skepticism about the danger of big government. Sensitized to the sufferings of others by his own grief over the loss of his brother, as senator, Kennedy allowed his own intuitive sympathy for the underdog to bring him into common cause with the underprivileged and outcast in American society.

In part, this newest concern was another reaction. Statistics showed that nearly 20 percent of Americans lived below what the government defined as poverty level. As leaders of the civil rights movement shifted their emphasis from legal protections to economic justice and concerned themselves increasingly with the problems of the black urban ghetto, poverty became a much-discussed issue. Johnson announced his intention to unleash a "war on poverty" and introduced a far-reaching legislative program, known as the Great Society, which included provisions for Medicare, job training, urban renewal, rent subsidies, and income supplements. Where Kennedy differed from other politicians was in the depth of his commitment and his ability to empathize and identify with the poor. He went to where the poor lived — the black ghettoes of Bedford-Stuyvesant and Harlem in his own state, the cabins of Chicano migrant workers in California's grape and lettuce fields, the squalid hovels of blacks in Mississippi, the ramshackle shacks of Appalachia, the Indian reservations of South Dakota — always exhibiting what Channing Phillips called a "fantastic ability to communicate hope to some pretty rejected people." In Congress he supported the Great Society programs while urging that more had to be done. He persuaded New York businessmen and industrialists to participate and invest in an innovative redevelopment plan for Bedford-Stuyvesant. The poor saw him as neither ruthless nor opportunistic. Cesar Chavez, leader of a labor movement among California's migrant fruit and vegetable pickers, believed simply that Kennedy "could see things through the eyes of the poor. . . . It was like he was ours." A newsman who traveled with him wrote, "No one who has seen Kennedy on an Indian reservation . . . or in the stinking hovels of Appalachia or seen him take the hand of a starving Negro child in the Mississippi Delta accuses him of acting."

Kennedy decried those who believed race relations and poverty were a southern problem. "I have been in tenements in Harlem in the past several weeks," he told a New York City audience in April 1965, "where the smell of rats was so strong it was difficult to stay there for five minutes, and where children slept with lights turned on their feet to discourage attacks. . . . Thousands do not flock to Harlem to protest these conditions, much less to change them." His empathy was unshaken by the rage that manifested itself in the rioting in the predominantly black Watts section of Los Angeles in August 1965, inaugurating what would be four successive summers of black discontent. As, in the words of the economist and politician Daniel Patrick Moynihan, "civil rights and poverty issues disappeared from presidential pronouncements, to be replaced by . . . euphemisms for the forcible suppression of black rage," Kennedy pointed out that "through the eyes of the young slumdweller . . . the world is a dark and hopeless place." Calls for law and order missed the point, he asserted: "There is no point in telling Negroes to obey the law. To many Negroes the law

> *All these places—Harlem, Watts, Southside—are riots waiting to happen.*
> —ROBERT KENNEDY
> 1966

is the enemy. In Harlem, in Bedford-Stuyvesant, it has almost always been used against them." Kennedy believed that "the violent youth of the ghetto is not simply protesting his condition, but making a destructive and self-defeating attempt to assert his worth and dignity as a human being — to tell us that although we may scorn his contribution, we must still respect his power."

Kennedy's message was particularly well received by the nation's young people. That constituency grew as Kennedy gradually moved into a position of opposition to the Johnson administration on the issue of the Vietnam War.

The United States had supported the government of South Vietnam against the nationalist and communist guerrillas of the National Liberation Front (NLF, also called the Vietcong) since the mid-1950s. The NLF's goal was the reunification of Vietnam (the country had been divided into North and South in 1954) under the control of the communist regime of North Vietnam. Under John Kennedy, the United States had increased its role by sending military advisers to assist the government of the beleaguered president of South Vietnam, Ngo Dinh Diem. Some historians also believe that the Kennedy administration — dismayed at the Diem regime's corruption and dictatorial methods, which had alienated much of its support and threatened to make a mockery of U.S. claims to be supporting democracy in Vietnam — approved the coup that overthrew Diem in November 1963. Believing that Vietnam represented a test case of the U.S. determination to stand up to communism and that the Southeast Asian nation was the first of a series of "dominoes" that would fall to communism should the United States fail to demonstrate a will to resist and vowing not to be the first American president to lose a war, Johnson increased the U.S. involvement there. American combat troops took the field against the Vietcong, and U.S. bombers attacked targets in North Vietnam. The U.S. presence escalated steadily. Troop strength grew from 23,000 at the end of 1964 to 525,000 in 1968. The U.S. death toll — small in comparison to the Vietnamese count — rose correspondingly. One hundred and twelve Americans died in Vietnam in 1964, 1,130 in 1965, 4,179 in 1966, and 7,482 in 1967. The Vietnamese countryside was devastated by the bombing and fighting, and the economy became heavily dependent on U.S. aid.

Initial opposition to the war in the United States was slight. When in August 1964 Johnson sought congressional approval for the Tonkin Gulf resolution, which authorized him to take "all steps necessary" in defense of South Vietnam's "freedom," only two senators — Ernest Gruening of Alaska and Wayne Morse of Oregon — opposed the measure. The resolution passed the House of Representatives unanimously. Even on college campuses, where opposition to the war received its most vociferous expression, 49 percent of students surveyed in May 1967 described themselves as hawks (supporters of the war). Only 35 percent described themselves as doves (opponents of the war).

Kennedy believed that the war was an unacceptable exercise of American power and that U.S. interests in Vietnam could be better served by negotiation. Nevertheless, while senators such as William Fulbright, George McGovern, and Eugene McCarthy were publicly expressing their opposition, Kennedy initially remained silent, aware that criticism of Johnson on his part would be dismissed as evidence of a personal vendetta against the president and of his own desire to fill that office. He also hesitated out of awareness of the role that his brother had played in initiating the U.S. involvement in Vietnam. In February 1966 he made his first public statement on the issue, saying that as the NLF would have to be part of any negotiations to end the war, it should be part of a coalition government for South Vietnam. The administration's reaction was harsh, with Vice-president Hubert Humphrey likening Kennedy's suggestion to "letting a fox in the chicken coop" or an arsonist in the fire department.

Kennedy's conviction that the war was immoral grew as the consequences of U.S. involvement grew and it became evident that Johnson had no intention of negotiating. The nightly news carried footage

Confused and frightened residents of the ancient Vietnamese city of Hue seek safety with U.S. Marines following a brief cessation in the street fighting that accompanied the Vietcong's Tet Offensive in early 1968. Tet convinced many Americans that Johnson's claim that the United States was nearing victory in Vietnam was misguided at best.

Vietnam was perhaps the best-documented war in this country's history. The daily newspaper and television coverage of the bloodshed and devastation in Vietnam helped turn American public opinion against the war. This photograph of a ravaged market area in Hue was taken in April 1968.

of wounded and demoralized U.S. troops, burned and ravaged Vietnamese hamlets, scores of refugees fleeing their devastated homes and fields, and the death count for the week so far. Unable to see the limited effectiveness of modern military technology in defeating a dedicated, well-organized guerrilla force that enjoyed a great deal of popular support, Johnson responded by sending more troops and bombs. Convinced, in Arthur Schlesinger's words, that "Johnson was hell-bent on smashing his way to military victory, was deluded as to victory's likelihood and indifferent as to its human consequences and, worst of all, had retreated into some realm beyond the reach of reasoned argument," Kennedy gave a major speech on the war in March 1967.

He began by accepting the blame, as a member of his brother's administration, for the U.S. involvement in Vietnam, then portrayed the war in terms of what it meant for the individual men and women

— most of them peasants — in Vietnam. Emphasizing that as the citizens of a democratic nation "we are all participants," Kennedy described the war as the "vacant moment of amazed fear as a mother and child watch death by fire fall from an improbable machine sent by a country they barely comprehend . . . the night of death destroying yesterday's promise of family and land and home." He said that the United States should halt the bombing and announce its willingness to negotiate. The perceived rightness of the U.S. cause was simply no justification for its cost in human suffering: "Although the world's imperfections may call forth the act of war, righteousness cannot obscure the agony and pain those acts bring to a single child." Finally, he condemned the U.S. actions in Vietnam as unworthy of the nation's higher sense of itself. "We are not in Vietnam to play the role of an avenging angel pouring death and destruction on the roads and factories and homes of a guilty land," he said, and went on to ask, "Can anyone believe this nation, with all its fantastic power and resources, will be endangered by a wise and magnanimous action toward a small and difficult adversary?"

Criticism from the Johnson administration and some of the press was again sharp. Kennedy was accused of being willing to sacrifice the blood of American soldiers to his own political ambition. Johnson stated that the North Vietnamese and NLF would only use a bombing halt as an opportunity to restrengthen themselves for further offensives. A Gallup poll taken in October 1967 revealed that 53 percent of Americans favored increased escalation. Needing more manpower, at the end of the year Johnson would bring an end to the deferments that exempted college students from the draft. The move increased opposition to the war on college campuses as well as among the upper and middle classes, whose sons were now more likely to be drafted and serve in Vietnam. The weekly death counts continued to mount. Although not a majority, those who opposed the war formed a large, vocal, and increasingly influential constituency, and Kennedy was emerging as their most prominent spokesman.

It was impossible for him not to tell the truth as he saw it. I think that is why some people thought he was ruthless. At times the truth is ruthless.
—AVERELL HARRIMAN
on Kennedy

7

Seeking a Newer World

Lyndon Johnson gave a major address on the Vietnam War in January 1968. He asserted that 65 percent of the South Vietnamese population was secure under military protection and assured the American people that the United States was winning the war. On the last day of that month the Vietcong and North Vietnamese launched the Tet Offensive, named after the Vietnamese holiday of the lunar new year. They quickly overran countless towns and villages, 64 district cities, 80 percent of the South Vietnamese provincial capitals, 12 U.S. bases, and the American embassy in Saigon, South Vietnam's capital. Shown nightly on the evening news, live footage of the offensive, particularly the fierce fighting around the embassy and in the ancient capital of Hue, stunned the American public. Johnson's assurances now seemed either delusions or lies. How could the United States claim to be winning the war when it was unable even to protect its own embassy? Even the shibboleth that the U.S. forces controlled the cities and the Vietcong controlled the countryside seemed to have been destroyed. It was now plain to many Americans that

LBJ's resistance to negotiation [on Vietnam] verges on a sort of madness.
—HENRY KISSINGER

Kennedy walks toward the Capitol after announcing that he was reassessing his decision not to seek the presidency in 1968. Kennedy worried that a challenge to Johnson would be seen as motivated solely by personal ambition rather than concern over the issues.

As U.S. involvement in Vietnam grew, so did domestic opposition to the war. This clash between antiwar demonstrators and military police outside the Pentagon in October 1967 was one of a number of such incidents that took place during the next five years.

victory, were it to come, was a long way off and could be achieved only at the cost of a great deal more American lives. With the end of the student deferments, no longer would those lives belong predominantly to minorities and members of the lower economic classes.

The war had been brought home to the middle class, many of whose members now joined with students and peace activists in demanding that Johnson either negotiate or find a way to end the war and bring the troops home. Antiwar demonstrations greeted virtually every public appearance Johnson or a ranking member of his administration made. Adding to the dissatisfaction with the Johnson presidency was the war's enormous cost, which combined with Johnson's expenditures for his

Great Society programs to create high inflation that reduced the purchasing power of most Americans.

On February 8, Kennedy delivered another speech on Vietnam. He spoke of the obvious failure of the U.S. mission there — "Half a million American soldiers, with 700,000 Vietnamese allies, with total command of the air, total command of the sea, backed by huge resources and the most modern weapons, are unable to secure even a single city from the attacks of an enemy whose total strength is about 250,000" — and declared that American dollars and resources would be better spent at home fighting poverty. "We can and should offer reasonable assistance to Asia," he stated, "but we cannot build a Great Society there if we cannot build one at home." The war was not winnable, Kennedy said, and he again advocated a political settlement that would allow the Vietcong — who were supported by a large percentage of the Vietnamese population — to participate in the political life of the nation. On March 7, from the Senate floor, he again condemned further escalation. He had now concluded that a unilateral withdrawal of U.S. troops was the best course but did not feel the time was right to make his position public.

With Johnson an increasingly divisive figure, a handful of liberal Democrats began searching for a candidate to challenge him for the party's nomination for the fall election. The most energetic and influential was Allard Lowenstein, a congressman and activist from Long Island, New York. Conventional political wisdom deemed the effort folly. The president was by definition the most powerful man in his party; his position provided him the opportunity to exert the type of influence that resulted in the loyalty of the governors, mayors, and local political organizations who would control delegates at the nominating convention. Adding to the enormity of what Lowenstein proposed was the fact that no politician was more adept at such horse trading than the shrewd Johnson. A candidate who took on the president and lost would do considerable damage to his political future.

Kennedy tells a Senate housing subcommittee in March 1968 that the administration's proposed housing program is inadequate. As the cost of the Vietnam War drew funding away from social welfare programs at home, Kennedy became increasingly critical of Johnson's domestic policy.

Eugene McCarthy meets the press the morning after the 1968 New Hampshire presidential primary. McCarthy had initially rejected the suggestion that he challenge Johnson but had eventually succumbed to activist Allard Lowenstein's pleas, saying, "There comes a time when an honorable man simply has to raise the flag."

Lowenstein saw things differently. He believed the time was ripe for a new politics, centered not on party loyalty and organization but on the issues — poverty, race relations, and the war — that were dividing America. By Lowenstein's reckoning, Johnson had alienated so much of his potential constituency that a candidate willing to run on a platform of opposition to the war might be able to wrest the nomination from him. He cited polls showing the president's diminishing support, particularly on the war issue. Nor did the premium the nominating process placed on the support of party leaders — most of whom would be expected, out of party loyalty, to support the incumbent president — faze Lowenstein. Democratic mayors, governors, and senators wanted one thing, he believed — to elect a Democratic president in November. If it could be demonstrated that an alternative candidate had more support among voters than Johnson, the party regulars would have little choice but to accept him as their nominee.

Lowenstein sought a candidate willing to demonstrate his popular support by challenging Johnson in the party primaries. His first choice was Kennedy, who was easily the most well known of the president's critics on the war, but the senator balked at the idea.

Kennedy recognized that the odds against a successful challenge for the nomination were immense. He cited a Gallup Poll taken immediately after Tet in which 61 percent of Americans described themselves as hawks (23 percent called themselves doves) and 70 percent were in favor of continued bombing. Successful or not, a bid by Kennedy for the nomination was likely to divide the Democrats and cost them whatever chance they held to win the election in November. Kennedy told friends that he did not wish to break with the party that had made his brother president. He was also keenly aware that a failed attempt might prove costly to his future political career, but his greatest worry was that his candidacy would be seen as motivated by personal ambition and harbored resentment against Johnson rather than concern over the issues and would prove as divisive as Johnson's presence in the race.

The passion Kennedy aroused in his supporters was matched by the vehemence of the dislike felt for him by his detractors, who still voiced the familiar criticisms. Many believed, in the words Gore Vidal had written five years earlier, that Kennedy's "obvious characteristics [were] energy, vindictiveness and a simple-mindedness about human motives which may yet bring him down." Remembering the accusatory counsel of the Rackets Committee, Vidal concluded that Kennedy would make a "dangerously authoritarian-minded president."

Kennedy's initial responses to Lowenstein's inquiries were negative. Even before Tet, in November 1967, Kennedy had determined, in Schlesinger's words, "that it would be a great mistake to challenge Johnson at this point — that it would be considered evidence of his ruthlessness, his ambition, and of a personal vendetta." One day before Tet he told a roomful of journalists at the National Press Club that he could not conceive of any circumstances under which he would seek the nomination. In truth, he had never really made up his mind, and the issues would not go away. There was Tet, and the way the war cut into funding for domestic social

Members of the Black Panther party, a radical black nationalist group, congregate outside the organization's school in the Fillmore district of San Francisco. As the civil rights movement grew more militant in the late 1960s, the Black Panthers and other groups advocated violent action against the government with the aim of creating a separate black nation.

Kennedy's late entrance into the 1968 presidential race left him with no organizations in place in the primary states. His campaign thus became a last-minute, improvisatory exercise based less on groundwork and planning than on demonstrating his popular support. Here he is greeted by backers upon his arrival in Fort Wayne, Indiana.

problems Kennedy regarded as important. He was also disturbed by the administration's rejection of the February 1968 report of the Kerner Commission on Civil Disorders, which warned that the United States was moving toward "two societies, one black, one white, separate but unequal" and recommended the introduction of massive federal economic and social welfare programs to end the "destruction of lives" that led to such polarization. Supporters urged him to run. Columnist Jack Newfield wrote in the *Village Voice*: "If Kennedy does not run in 1968, the best side of his character will die. . . . It will die every time a kid asks him, if he is so much against the Vietnam War, how come he is putting party above principle? It will die every time a stranger quotes his own words back to him on the value of courage."

While Kennedy wavered, a disappointed Lowenstein found another candidate, Senator Eugene McCarthy of Minnesota, who was also a Catholic opposed to the war but lacked the New York senator's national stature. Overjoyed to have a standard-bearer, thousands of young antiwar students eager to offer their services to the McCarthy campaign descended on New Hampshire, scene of the first primary, where the more hirsute among them were urged to shave, cut their hair, and "get clean for Gene." McCarthy's entrance complicated Kennedy's decision, for he regarded the intellectual Minnesotan as a smart but lazy senator inclined to pander to corporate interest groups and with an unenlightened record on social issues. Kennedy believed that McCarthy's apparent unconcern with questions other than the war and patrician disregard for social and economic issues made him unfit for the presidency.

On March 12, the date of the New Hampshire primary, McCarthy earned 42.4 percent of the popular vote to 49.5 percent for Johnson, a result that was generally interpreted as a presidential defeat for the depth of antiwar and anti-Johnson sentiment it revealed. In the meantime, Kennedy continued to agonize over entering the race. Two days after the primary, Johnson rejected Kennedy's proposal of a bipartisan commission to examine U.S. policy in Vietnam, a decision that Kennedy said made it "unmistakably clear to me that so long as Lyndon Johnson was president our Vietnam policy would consist of only more war, more troops, more killing and more senseless destruction of the country we were supposedly there to save. That night I decided to run for president." Schlesinger and others believe he had made his decision to run a week or so earlier.

Kennedy's announcement, which he gave on March 16, in the same room of the Senate office building where his brother had announced eight years earlier, brought a storm of criticism. His timing could not have been worse. Now Kennedy was not only ruthless and opportunistic, but he lacked the courage to challenge Johnson and entered only when McCarthy demonstrated the president's vul-

> *His reputation was for ruthlessness, yet in 1968 there seemed no major political figure whose image so contrasted with the reality; most politicians seem attractive from a distance but under closer examinations they fade; the vanities, the pettiness, the vulgarities come out. Robert Kennedy was different. Under closer inspection he was far more winning than most.*
> —DAVID HALBERSTAM
> journalist and author,
> May 1968

Kennedy campaigns in Sioux Falls, South Dakota. He wished, he said, to end the many divisions in the nation, but the 1968 presidential campaign demonstrated instead just how badly polarized American society had become.

nerability. Not only was he willing to split the Democratic party, but he was dividing the Democratic antiwar vote, thereby ensuring Johnson's nomination. Although he was expecting criticism, its vehemence hurt Kennedy, but the reception at Kansas State University, his first campaign stop, was quite different. There he told a large and wildly enthusiastic crowd, "Every night we watch horror on the evening news. Violence spreads inexorably across the nation, filling our streets and crippling our lives. . . . Can we ordain to ourselves the awful majesty of God — to decide what cities and villages are to be destroyed, who will live and who will die, and who will join the refugees wandering in a desert of our own creation? . . . In these next eight months, we are going to decide what this country will stand for — and what kind of men we are." Columnist Jimmy Breslin described the clamor of his supporters to touch him at the airport following his appearance: "They tore at Robert Kennedy. They tore the buttons from his shirt-cuffs. . . . They tore at his suit-buttons. They reached for his hair and his face. He went down the fence, hands out, his body swaying backwards so that they could not claw him in the face, and the people on the other side of the fence grabbed his hands and tried to pull him to them." Veteran campaign writers marveled at this display of hysteria on the part of reputedly staid Kansans.

Stunned by McCarthy's success, Kennedy's entrance into the race, a Gallup Poll showing that only 26 percent of Americans approved of his handling of the war, calls from the House of Representatives for a congressional review of the United States's Vietnam policy, and the advice of his top aides and advisers that the war was essentially unwinnable and that he should lower the level of American involvement, Johnson announced on March 31 that he would not be a candidate for president.

Kennedy's whirlwind campaign — a true exercise in the new politics — followed. There was little evidence of the vaunted Kennedy machine. He had no organization ready, the support of few party politicians, and no delegate slates pledged to him. But everywhere there were the crowds, aching to touch him, tumultuous and supportive through Nebraska and Indiana, smaller and less enthusiastic in Oregon, where McCarthy denigrated Kennedy supporters as the "less-intelligent and less well-educated voters of the country," wild and outsized again in California. There were his soothing words the night of King's assassination, his flight to Atlanta for King's funeral, the hand-lettered signs of support in the black ghettoes (Kennedy White but All Right read a typical one), his calls for a coalition of working-class whites and blacks to "really turn this country around," the brilliant speech in Cleveland shortly after King's death asking for an end not only to individual violence but the "violence of institutions, [of] indifference and inaction and slow decay . . . that affects the poor [and] poisons relations between the races . . . [the violence that is the] slow destruction of a child by hunger and a school without books and homes without heat in the winter." There were the pledges to end the divisions in the country, to end poverty, to end the war, and always the literary allusions — usually to Shaw, and the hope of achieving "things that never were"; oftentimes to the British poet Alfred Lord Tennyson: "Come, my friends/'Tis not too late to seek a newer world." There were the visits to black ghettoes and working-class enclaves in Gary, Indiana, and Los Angeles, to Sioux Indian reservations in South Dakota, to the camps of migrant workers in Delano, California, and everywhere the stunning turnout of minorities and the poor for Kennedy on primary day. There were the victories in Nebraska and Indiana, the defeat in Oregon, and the final triumph in California, with a joyous Kennedy vowing to chase Humphrey's "ass all over the country" in quest of the nomination, his supporters exultant in celebration, certain the nomination was his, until gunshots fired by a young Jordanian American named Sirhan Sirhan in the kitchen of Los Angeles's Ambassador Hotel brought the 85-day crusade to an end.

> *The building of a truly integrated society depends on the development of economic self-sufficiency and security in the communities of poverty, for only then will the residents of these areas have the wherewithal to move freely within the society.*
> —ROBERT KENNEDY

8

"Things That Never Were"

An ambulance carried Robert Kennedy to Central Receiving Hospital, where he received emergency treatment, and then to the Hospital of the Good Samaritan, which was better suited for the complicated surgery he required. Kennedy had been shot three times. Bullets were imbedded in his neck and midbrain; a third had grazed his forehead. At the Ambassador Hotel the crowd in the Embassy Room dispersed. Some scattered groups of two and three people, seeking to console one another, remained. Men and women wept and cursed in the hotel's hallways and the parking lots outside. Others passed by one another too stunned to speak. The black civil rights leader Charles Evers, who would later say that "Bobby Kennedy was the last white man in America who could bring peace between the races," sat alone on the front steps. He would remain there until after sunrise.

> *Good luck is something you make and bad luck is something you endure.*
> —ROBERT KENNEDY

A London policeman learns of Kennedy's shooting. For many, Kennedy's death, coming so soon after the murder of Martin Luther King, Jr., confirmed what the historian Garry Wills called a sense that "man had not merely lost control of his history, but might never regain it."

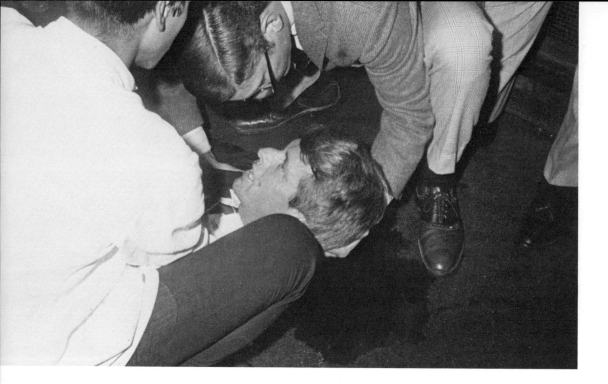

A severely wounded Robert Kennedy, moments after the shooting.

Kennedy went into surgery shortly after 3:00 A.M. on the morning of June 5. Ignoring the bullet in his neck, which was not considered life threatening, doctors removed all but a fragment of the bullet in his brain, but the damage had been severe. While the nation waited and prayed, Kennedy lingered in a coma for more than 25 hours. He was pronounced dead early in the morning of June 6.

An airplane carried his body to New York City, where a funeral mass was to be celebrated at St. Patrick's Cathedral. As the hearse and motorcade made its way from the airport to the church, the streets and highway overpasses were lined with people come to pay their last respects. In the city's Hispanic neighborhoods mourners held aloft hand-drawn banners emblazoned simply *Viva!* (He lives!). At the cathedral more than 7,000 people waited for the senator. It was shortly after 9:00 in the evening; throughout the sultry night the crowd grew, until at 5:30 the following morning, when the cathedral was opened, the line of mourners stretched for blocks. For hours they filed inside past the closed coffin to say farewell. Most remained silent; some reached out to touch the casket; others whispered,

"Good-bye, Bobby." Occasionally a mourner broke down and wept aloud. Outside, newcomers continued to join the line, undeterred by reports that the wait was two, then five, hours long. Some were overcome by the day's stifling heat, and the New York City Fire Department ordered hydrants on the street opened to provide drinking water. In the cooler darkness of the cathedral, priests said the day's schedule of eight masses as the mourners continued to file in. Friends and family members stood honor guard near Kennedy's coffin, many fondly recalling better times and the personal side of the public figure: the deeply affectionate father at home amid the warm chaos of Hickory Hill, where the din of his 10 children and countless pets filled the air; the still young man possessed of an "insolent fatalism about life," driven to test himself physically through mountain climbing, white-water rafting, and skiing and fond of quoting the American philosopher and poet Ralph Waldo Emerson: "It was high counsel that I once heard given to a young person, 'Always do what you are afraid to do' "; the thousand large and small generosities that led his friends Kenneth O'Donnell and David Powers to remember, "Always he was the kindest man we ever knew."

More than 1 million grieving Americans lined the route of the Kennedy funeral train as it made its way from New York to Washington.

The church was scheduled to close at ten, but still the mourners came, all through the night. The following morning, June 8, Archbishop Terence Cooke and Richard Cardinal Cushing said the funeral mass. Twenty-three hundred invited guests filled the church, among them some of America's most prominent political, social, and cultural figures. Lyndon Johnson and his wife sat opposite the Kennedy family; Eugene McCarthy buried his head in his hands. Edward Kennedy, Robert's younger brother and the last surviving son of Joseph and Rose, himself a senator from Massachusetts, gave the eulogy, asking that his brother "not be idealized, or enlarged in death beyond what he was in life, [but] remembered simply as a good and decent man, who saw wrong and tried to right it, saw suffering and tried to heal it, saw war and tried to stop it."

As the coffin was loaded aboard the hearse, mourners jammed Fifth Avenue on both sides of the street for 20 blocks, paying silent tribute as the motorcade made its way to Pennsylvania Station. A 21-car train carried Kennedy to Washington, D.C. Huge crowds pressed along the tracks on the train's route. Observers were again struck by the preponderance of black faces. Many mourners were bearing signs of eloquent testimony to their grief — We Have Lost Our Last Hope, or Pray For Us, Bobby. As the train rolled through the countryside, away from the cities and towns, those on board saw small somber clusters of three and four people waiting patiently at trackside, gently waving small American flags as the funeral train passed by. In Baltimore a huge, mostly black crowd joined hands and sang the "Battle Hymn of the Republic" as the train pulled in. All told, 1 million people lined the 226 miles of track between New York and Washington to bid Kennedy farewell.

Robert Kennedy was buried 20 yards from his brother in Arlington National Cemetery on June 8, 1968. His 11th child, a daughter, Rory, was born several months after his death. In a Chicago amphitheater in August Hubert Humphrey won the Democratic nomination for president while on the streets outside thousands of antiwar demonstrators were beaten and arrested in what a commission of inquiry later termed a "police riot." Humphrey went on to lose the election to the Republican candidate, Richard Nixon. That year 16,511 Americans died in Vietnam. Opposition to the war grew, reaching a crisis point in May 1970 with the fatal shootings of four student protesters by the Ohio National Guard on the campus of Kent State University. One year later the administration jailed more than 13,000 antiwar demonstrators without charges in Washington, D.C., holding many in the city's football stadium. By the time the United States withdrew its forces from Vietnam in 1973, more than 59,000 Americans had been killed there, more than 1.5 million Vietnamese civilians had lost their lives, millions more were homeless refugees, and the United States had dropped more than 3 times the bomb

Kennedy strolls along the Oregon coast with his dog Freckles in May 1968. His greatest appeal was always among young people. Twenty years after their death, Robert Kennedy and Martin Luther King, Jr., were named the two most admired public figures, living or dead, in a nationwide poll of American youth.

tonnage on that country as it had dropped in all of World War II. The damage to the neighboring nation of Cambodia was possibly even greater. Nixon dismantled the social programs of the Great Society, unleashed a program of domestic surveillance that outdid the excesses of the FBI in the Hoover era, and ultimately resigned in disgrace in August 1974 for a series of affronts to the letter and spirit of the Constitution. He left behind him a nation discouraged about the possibility of successfully using the political system to effect significant social change and a profound feeling of disillusionment acurately characterized by pollster Louis Harris as "a veritable floodtide of disenchantment, seemingly gaining momentum with each passing year." The percentage of eligible voters who actually cast a ballot in the 1976 election was the lowest since 1948, giving way to an era in which it seemed, according to the historian William Leuchtenburg, "as though America had rolled back a quarter of a century of its history."

Further Reading

Burner, David, and Thomas R. West. *The Torch Is Passed: The Kennedy Brothers and American Liberalism.* New York: Atheneum, 1984.

David, Lester, and Irene David. *Bobby Kennedy: The Making of a Folk Hero.* New York: Dodd, Mead, 1986.

DeToledano, Ralph. *R.F.K.* New York: Putnam, 1967.

Graves, Charles Parlin. *Robert Kennedy: Man Who Dared to Dream.* Champaign, IL: Garrard, 1970.

Guthman, Edwin. *We Band of Brothers.* New York: Harper & Row, 1971.

Halberstam, David. *The Unfinished Odyssey of Robert Kennedy.* New York: Random House, 1968.

Kennedy, Robert F. *Robert Kennedy In His Own Words: The Unpublished Recollections of the Kennedy Years.* Edited by Edwin O. Guthman and Jeffrey Shulman. New York: Bantam, 1988.

———. *Thirteen Days: A Memoir of the Cuban Missile Crisis.* New York: Norton, 1969.

Kimball, Penn. *Bobby Kennedy and the New Politics.* Englewood Cliffs, NJ: Prentice-Hall, 1968.

Koch, Thilo. *Fighters for a New World.* New York: Putnam, 1969.

Lasky, Victor. *Robert Kennedy: The Myth and the Man.* New York: Trident, 1968.

Navasky, Victor S. *Kennedy Justice.* New York: Atheneum, 1971.

Newfield, Jack. *Robert Kennedy: A Memoir.* New York: Dutton, 1969.

Randall, Marta. *John F. Kennedy.* New York: Chelsea House, 1988.

Ross, Douglas. *Robert F. Kennedy: Apostle of Change.* New York: Trident, 1968.

Schoor, Gene. *Young Robert Kennedy.* New York: McGraw-Hill, 1969.

Shannon, William Vincent. *The Heir Apparent.* New York: Macmillan, 1967.

Sorensen, Theodore C. *The Kennedy Legacy.* New York: Macmillan, 1969.

Stein, Jean. *American Journey.* New York: Harcourt Brace Jovanovich, 1970.

Steinberg, Alfred. *The Kennedy Brothers.* New York: Putnam, 1969.

Wills, Gary. *The Kennedy Imprisonment.* Boston: Little, Brown, 1982.

Witcover, Jules. *85 Days.* New York, Putnam, 1969.

Wofford, Harris. *Of Kennedys and Kings.* New York: Farrar, Straus & Giroux, 1980.

Chronology

Nov. 20, 1925	Born Robert Francis Kennedy in Brookline, Massachusetts
1946	Enlists in the Navy
March 1948	Graduates from Harvard University
1948	Tours Europe and the Middle East
June 1950	Marries Ethel Skakel
June 1951	Graduates from the University of Virginia Law School
1951	Takes a position at the U.S. Justice Department
1952	Manages John Kennedy's campaign for the Senate; becomes minority assistant counsel for the Senate Subcommittee on Investigations
1953	Resigns from subcommittee
1954	Returns to subcommittee; serves as minority counsel
Nov. 1954	Elections return Democratic Senate majority; Kennedy becomes majority counsel
1955	Kennedy tours the Soviet Union with Supreme Court Justice William O. Douglas
1956	Serves as a delegate to the Democratic National Convention in Chicago; joins Adlai Stevenson's campaign as an adviser; after Stevenson's defeat, returns to work in the Senate as chief counsel of the Rackets Committee
Sept. 1959	Resigns from the Rackets Committee in order to manage John Kennedy's presidential campaign
Nov. 1960	John Kennedy wins the election; appoints Robert Kennedy attorney general
April 17, 1961	United States sponsors an invasion of Cuba at the Bay of Pigs
Oct. 1962	Cuban missile crisis
Aug. 1963	March on Washington
Nov. 22, 1963	John Kennedy is assassinated
Nov. 1964	Kennedy is elected to the United States Senate
Aug. 1965	Race riots break out in the Watts section of Los Angeles
March 7, 1968	Kennedy publicly condemns further escalation of the Vietnam War
March 16, 1968	Declares his candidacy for the presidency
April 4, 1968	Martin Luther King, Jr., is assassinated
June 4, 1968	Kennedy is shot
June 6, 1968	Dies at the Hospital of the Good Samaritan

Index

Daniel J. Petrillo is a professor of history at a southern university, where he specializes in recent American history. A former instructor at Yale University, he is the author of numerous books and articles.

Arthur M. Schlesinger, jr., taught history at Harvard for many years and is currently Albert Schweitzer Professor of the Humanities at City University of New York. He is the author of numerous highly praised works in American history and has twice been awarded the Pulitzer Prize. He served in the White House as special assistant to Presidents Kennedy and Johnson.

PICTURE CREDITS